S0-CCE-895

Croc and the Fox

By

Eve Langlais

Copyright © August 2012, Eve Langlais
Cover Art by Amanda Kelsey © August 2012
Content Edited by Brandi Buckwine

Produced in Canada
Published by Eve Langlais
1606 Main Street, PO Box 151, Stittsville, Ontario, Canada,
K2S1A3

www.EveLanglais.com

ISBN-13: 978-1478357575

ISBN-10: 1478357576

Croc and the Fox is a work of fiction and the characters, events and
dialogue found within the story are of the author's imagination and
are not to be construed as real. Any resemblance to actual events or
persons, either living or deceased, is completely coincidental.
No part of this book may be reproduced or shared in any form or by
any means, electronic or mechanical, including but not limited to
digital copying, file sharing, audio recording, email and printing
without permission in writing from the author.

Chapter One

Early morning, at Moreau Island Industries…

Forget the experimental drugs killing her, boredom would get her first. Breakfast eaten – lukewarm mush again, yay – teeth brushed – with the hem of her gown because the guards feared them making a shank out of toothbrushes, whatever that meant – she'd even finished her daily walk – a dozen turns around her tiny cell. Morning routine completed, she now had the whole day ahead of her. That sucked. With nothing better to do, Project counted the cracks decorating the walls of her cell again. Sure, she already knew the answer – five thousand, three hundred and forty one – but it beat counting the bars – a measly twelve – which she finished too quickly.

What a slow week. No new prisoners for her to gawk at and eagerly question about the outside world. No hallucinatory drugs giving her the pasties or helping her see pretty rainbows. Not a single jab with an electrified cattle prod. Nothing. *I feel so underappreciated.* What did a prisoner need to do to get some attention from an evil doctor?

At this point in her doldrums, she would have even welcomed the unsmiling countenance of Fred, the guard. Not that his presence boded well since it meant someone usually wanted to poke her with sharp objects. Still though, a girl liked to feel wanted, even if only for experiments.

It seemed like forever since any of the mad scientists took her out to run tests – she beat the mice in the maze every time – or got her to chug some new,

3

steaming concoction. Lest you misunderstand, it wasn't that she enjoyed those times – the needles were painful, the electric shock therapy left her trembling, and the potions she swallowed tasted vile – but she couldn't deny getting treated like a lab rat broke up the boredom of her current status. Locked in a room only slighter wider than she was tall, there just wasn't much for a girl to do.

Unlike the other occupants in the holding area, she didn't give in to screaming – it made her head hurt – or banging her noggin on the wall – which also gave her a wicked headache. But given the lack of amenities, some form of entertainment was needed. Televisions weren't allowed in their cells anymore because some of the prisoners used them as weapons. Books ended up banned years ago, mostly because they jammed up the toilets when people used them to wipe their bottoms. Drawing on the walls with her bodily fluids, like blood, pee and feces? Talk about an *ick* factor and totally not her thing. What did that leave? Not much to entertain her mind.

So, she counted things. Constantly.

One. Two. Three. She'd reached seven hundred and thirty one cracks when the first rumble shook the walls. She didn't pay it much attention. Every few months, something blew up in the labs. Lucky for her, she wasn't present when that happened, but she couldn't say as much for some of the others. Poor Project M87 never was the same when he returned without his left arm and one of his eyes.

Seven hundred and thirty two. Thirty three. Again, the room around her shuddered, followed by the faint blaring of alarms. *Uh-oh, someone is going to be in trouble.* She could always determine the severity of a screw up by the turnover in staff. Failure wasn't tolerated.

The rumbles continued and the wailing of sirens increased. Around her, in the flanking cells, the other inhabitants perked up, coming to their bars to peek, craning to hear the vague commotion so far overhead. To her surprise, the chaos got louder. Odd, because just overhead were the storage levels, an added buffer between the projects and the experimental labs. What had the scientists done this time to create such havoc?

Cracking sounds. Screams. More shaking of the walls. And for the first time ever, the sirens in their section lit with a red whirling light and ululating screech. How exciting.

The end was nigh. Or so the misshapen creature in cell number twenty-nine began to scream.

"We're all gonna die!" yelled the monster, who was half-man, half-melted monstrosity. "Me first! Please!"

"Get in line," warbled the amphibious prisoner in the cell across from hers. "I've been here longer than you. I should go first."

Actually, Project was the longest living inhabitant of the dungeon, but she kept that to herself, not wanting to draw their jealousy. *I am the queen of experimental torture. Yay for me!*

Up and down the corridor, people shouted their right to die first. Project didn't add her voice. Life as a prisoner might suck, but still, who said death would be an improvement? Surely there existed more to the world than an endless series of sterile labs, concrete cells, nondescript corridors and men in white coats? Not everyone lived in a locked room, and according to the books she'd read, before the doctors took them away, a whole world existed outside the lab, a vast place where a shifter could live, free of rules and rounds of blood-work.

Amelie, who used to occupy the cell alongside hers, spoke wistfully of the life she left behind. When their guards served gruel, Amelie used to stare at it and cry about how much she missed McDonald's. *Wasn't he the guy who owned a farm?* Still, despite some of her obvious off the wall observations, Project loved to listen to Amelie and the other captives tell their stories. Tall tales about how outside the lab there were no doctors in white coats waiting to do tests, or guards kicking over their bowls of mush, and where the toilet paper didn't scrape a bottom raw.

Okay, so Project believed in fairytales. It helped pass the time.

It took a while – two thousand, seven hundred and sixty one seconds to be precise – before the popping sounds and screams stopped. The building ceased its shudders, but the sirens still spun with a macabre red light while wailing. As melodies went, she preferred the occasional screaming.

And then, the alarm stopped. Dead silence took its place as even the prisoners clammed up, everyone straining to hear something. The lack of any noise proved even worse than the blaring horn.

The click and metallic clang of the door unlocking at the far end of the row saw her stepping back from the cell's only opening. Trepidation weaved its icy tendrils through her frame and she chewed her lower lip. Who came?

Usually in an emergency, the inhabitants of the dungeon were the last to get checked on, the prisoners considered expendable. Something about this whole scenario didn't seem right.

The thump of feet – *one, two, three…* – signaled someone came.

"Oh my god, he's got a gun," an inmate screamed.

"And he's covered in blood."

"Welcome, death. I've been waiting," blubbered the blob.

None of the comments inspired confidence, and Project took another step back.

"Holy freaking nightmare!" The curse, uttered in a gravelly voice sent shivers down her spine. She didn't recognize the owner of the voice, another bad sign.

Feeling suddenly faint, she huddled into a ball in the corner of her cell, trying to drown out the echoing pops that preceded the clank and creak of bars being swung open, the muttered expletives, the harsh sobs as her cellmates met the man with the deep voice. *Has death finally come for us?*

Project squeezed her eyes tight and clenched her fists, straining to call her other shape.

Go-go, shapeshifting animal. She sighed, as once again, she flunked Morphing 101. *I am the most pathetic shapeshifter ever.* It seemed her lack of ability to switch meant she would meet death without even a chance to fight. Her own fault, she guessed. *I did wish for some excitement.* But still, this was kind of extreme. She would have settled for a book.

*

Viktor shot the lock off the last cell, already cringing at what he'd probably find inside. The other locked and dank rooms with their contents would haunt him forever, the occupants, pitiful experiments gone wrong. Horribly wrong. Any semblance to humanity, any remnant of sanity, long gone. *The mastermind will pay for this.*

At least now, the prisoners, blubbering messes who kept begging him to kill them, could get the help they needed. Everyone owed a big round of thanks to the FUC agent who deciphered the riddle of the mastermind's location. Jessie, their resident swan geek and tech expert, was the one who discovered Moreau Island Industries.

On the surface, the establishment seemed legit, a laboratory for the testing and creation of hemorrhoid medication and cough syrup. But, a furtive investigation of the premises showed large numbers of shifters and mercenaries, disguised as guards, scattered about. FUC – which stood for Furry United Coalition, a group of shapeshifters dedicated to protecting their kind – along with the Avian Airforce – led by Jessie's dad, the swan king – mobilized their forces and struck within days of verification.

Less than an hour ago, Viktor led the troops into the ground fight to capture the hidden lab. He, and the others under his command, battled the human mercenaries. Killed the renegade shifters, and found a nightmare under several hidden levels of basements.

What kind of shifter experimented and tortured his own kind? The mastermind did, that was who. Yet, once again, FUC arrived too late to apprehend the foul villain. *But he can't run forever.* One day, the mastermind would slip up, and they'd pounce on the bastard, putting an end to his evil regime once and for all.

In the meantime, though, they had victims to help. Even now he could hear the gasps of surprise and murmurs of pity as some of the agents filtered into the basement prison. He only hoped they had enough room to transport them all.

Viktor swung open the final door in the macabre dungeon and braced himself for another nightmare. The lack of stench surprised him. All the other cells stank of waste and rot. Perhaps they'd cleaned this one out, their victim mercifully succumbing to the call of death.

A step into the room and at first he thought it empty, until he caught a whisper of movement. Turning his head to the left, he noted a huddled form in the corner lift a head crowned with tangled red curls and a gaze that glowed, bright and golden. The eyes blinked, and even though he couldn't see the face for the mess of hair, Viktor found himself enthralled with the luminous beauty of the orbs peering at him.

"Can you talk?" he asked when the female, had to be with those long lashes, kept staring at him. "It's okay. You're safe now. I've come to rescue you."

"Safe?" She spoke the word questioningly. Perhaps she didn't believe rescue had finally arrived.

"Yes, safe."

"Are you…" She paused, her soft voice fading. She scrambled to her feet, a dirty gown falling to her knees and molding to curves that raised her from his first impression of a child to woman, a tall woman, who just about matched him in height. Viktor forced his gaze from her shapely frame to her face with its delicate features. She lifted her pointed chin, some of her hair falling away from a grubby face adorned with a pert nose and full lips. Staring him boldly in the eye, she said, "Are you my father?"

God, he hoped not, because that would make his body's response totally inappropriate. Sanity reaffirmed itself. "Of course I'm not your father. Don't you remember who you are?"

She cocked her head. "I am Project X081."

He recoiled from the impersonal tag she used. "But what about before they began experimenting on you? What was your name then?"

A frown creased her brow. "Before? I was born here. Have always lived here."

The very idea appalled him. He held out his hand. "Come with me then, and see what freedom is."

Slender fingers slipped into his and Viktor almost yanked his hand away as awareness of her slammed into him. He fought it as he led her back through the dungeon housing so many failures and one sexy enigma. He let her tuck into him when they passed other agents as they searched the compound for clues.

Just before the exit, Viktor stopped and said grandly, "Welcome to the real world." He flung the emergency side door open and let the sunshine in.

His mystery lady took one look at the vast green field, the blue sky, and the sunshine. Then, she turned and ran back the way they came, shrieking in terror.

Chapter Two

Project ran blindly, her eyes still stinging from the brilliant light in the vast blue sky. Or at least, she assumed it was a sky. While having never seen it before, she'd read about it and scoffed at its existence. Raised in a world with a ceiling she could see and almost touch, who knew such a thing existed? It was even bigger than she could have imagined. And scary.

Unused to so much open space, the air laced with so many smells, Project panicked and did the only thing her frightened mind could handle. She went back to her cell to hide.

But she didn't flee alone.

The man who'd arrived to her rescue – a tall god with sharp features, a stern gaze and a hard body encased in black armor – followed her. While he didn't engage her in conversation on their race, he did bark at others, dressed in similar clothes, when they would have stepped into their path.

"Clear the way! Let her through. I've got this."

Bare fleet slapping, her breath coming in harsh pants, Project begged to differ. Scurrying down the stairs, because the elevator would have caused her to stop and wait, she heard the steady thump of his boots as he trailed her. She followed her scent trail through the unknown areas, rooms and hallways, she'd never seen. Arriving at long last at her familiar level, her home, she sprinted the last few yards and dove into her cell. Grabbing her blanket, she ducked under it. Body shivering, she hid, and hoped the man would go away.

"What are you doing?" His gravelly voice sounded right behind her.

She didn't answer. If she didn't speak, maybe he wouldn't see her hiding.

"Do you want to talk about what just happened?"

Talk about what? She was going to pretend the endless sky didn't exist. It was just a hallucination similar to the one brought on by those mushrooms the scientists fed her once.

"You can't hide in here forever."

Watch me.

*

Trembles racked the woman's body as she knelt on the floor, her head buried under a blanket. She'd wrapped her arms over it and had her bottom pushed up, revealing the edges of her rounded ass cheeks.

Viktor scratched his head. *What the hell?* One minute, she'd seemed so cooperative, following him like a docile lamb, the next, she bolted like a frightened doe chased by a tiger. Or in this case, a croc.

And all because he'd shown her freedom.

He tried to proceed gently. A victim, she didn't deserve the sharp edge of his tongue, but dammit, his patience rapidly waned. "My name is Viktor by the way. I'm a FUC agent, and I just want to help you."

She didn't reply.

"You can't hide under that blanket forever."

"I'm not hiding under the blanket."

Hunh? "You know I can see you?"

The edge of the tattered fabric lifted and a golden eye perused him. "You can?"

"Yeah."

"Oh." She sat up, crossed her legs and let her fingers play with the hem of her gown. "Hailey said it would work."

"Who's Hailey?"

"Cell block seven. She says in the wild, if danger came looking, she just stuck her head in the sand to hide."

"She did, did she?"

His mystery lady, who seemed to have more screws loose than he first thought, nodded enthusiastically. "Yup." Her smile fell. "But it didn't work with you."

"I doubt it works on anyone with a pair of eyes," he said with a snort.

"I should have known better than to listen to a bird. The guards are always saying how flighty they are."

He almost laughed until he realized she meant it quite seriously. "Since you're not hiding anymore, care to explain what happened outside?"

"I didn't like it." Her nose wrinkled in distaste.

"Didn't like what?"

"The sky. The bright light."

"Why not? Are you a nocturnal shifter?"

She shook her head.

He frowned, and she recoiled. It annoyed him. "I'm not going to hurt you. I'm just trying to understand why you're so scared."

"It's too big out there."

Ah, agoraphobia, a fear of open spaces. "It just seems that way because you've been imprisoned. You'll get used to it."

She shook her head sending wild locks flying. "No thanks. I'd rather not."

13

His jaw probably dropped a foot. "What do you mean, you'd rather not? You have to. You can't stay in this prison forever."

Her head tilted and she shot him a curious glance. "Why not?"

"What do you mean why not?" he sputtered. "This is a cell. Normal people don't want to live in cells. It's not right."

"Well I do."

"You can't."

Her lower lip jutted. "Oh yes I can."

She draped the blanket over her head and crossed her arms, her whole stance screaming stubborn.

"Now what are you doing?" he asked, no longer bothering to hide his exasperation.

"Ignoring you."

"You've got to be freaking kidding me. I order you to come with me."

"No."

"You can't say no. I'm in charge here."

"We've already ascertained you're not my father, nor a scientist, or a guard, which means I don't have to listen to you."

And then she clapped her hands over her ears and began to hum.

Screw this. Tired of talking with an obvious mad woman, Viktor leaned down and tore the blanket off. Before she could react, he scooped up the crazy redhead, upending her over his shoulder. She let out a squeak of surprise.

"What are you doing? Put me down."

"No." Arm locked over her thighs, her weight nothing on his bulky shoulder, he exited the cell.

"Where are we going?"

"Away from here."

"Are you taking me to the labs?"

"Of course not."

"Locking me in solitary?"

His jaw tightened. "No one will be locking you up, ever again." Well, unless she broke the law, but he'd let someone else explain that to her when – and if – they ever released her to the world at large.

"So where are we going then?"

"Like I said, away from here."

"But I don't want to leave."

"Too bad. I say you have to. And since I'm bigger than you, what I say goes." A childish retort for her juvenile arguing.

"This is kidnapping."

"Rescue," he corrected.

"You can't do this."

"I can and am." He jogged up the several flights of stairs, ignoring the strange looks he got from the other FUC operatives wandering the place, photographing and boxing anything they found of interest. He also ignored the former prisoner's demands to put her down. To go away. And to do something anatomically impossible with himself.

"Where did you learn such language?" he finally asked, reaching the top level. The vulgarity of her speech, especially coming from such a delicate looking cutie, surprised him.

"The guards. The doctors. The others in the cells with me. I even know some of them in Spanish. Would you like to hear them?" she replied sweetly.

"Sure, my boys could stand to learn some new ones. Feel free to shout as many as you like because we're going outside now."

"No!" she yelled. Viktor stumbled as she buried her face in his lower back and wrapped her arms around

15

his middle, tighter than the anaconda he dated a few years back.

"Can't breathe," he joked.

Her grip didn't loosen in the slightest. Faced with a dilemma, Viktor didn't immediately exit the building. If this were a soldier, or agent, acting like a great big wuss bag, he would have ignored the terror and thrown them out to meet the source. But, his mystery lady was a victim. Somehow he doubted Kloe, or his coworkers, would approve of him just tossing her into the sunshine given her fear. And, a teensy tiny part of him, didn't want to scare her further. A tiny part.

What to do? Maybe if he asked nicely, which went totally against all his training, she'd cooperate. "Could you please let go?"

She shook her head against his lower back and clung tighter.

Ordered? "Let me go now!"

Another shake.

Someone behind him snickered. This was getting ridiculous. No more Mr. Nice Croc. "You asked for it." Viktor slapped his hand on the rounded buttocks nestled so close to his face. The sharp crack echoed loudly as his palm met her barely covered flesh, but he tempered the strength behind the blow. Still, it had the desired effect.

She reared up with a screeched, "Ow!" and he swiveled her off his shoulder and onto her feet. But when she would have bolted, he manacled her wrists with one hand.

It didn't stop her from twisting and turning, fighting his grip and intention. "Let me go, you bully. You can't make me go out there."

"Yes I can," he stated calmly. He pulled her along, her bare feet sliding on the marbled floor to the glass doors leading outside. She cursed him out. Dug her heels in. It didn't stop him from reaching the portal and kicking it open.

A shriek left her lips that made his ears ring and she reversed strategies. Instead of fighting him, she suddenly threw herself at him, jumped on his body, forcing him to release her hands to catch her. Freed, she wrapped her legs around his waist, her arms around his neck and buried her face against his shoulder. Short of a pry bar, he doubted he'd get her off.

Sigh. *Why me?*

Viktor braced an arm around her middle, leaving his other one free to hold up a middle finger to Mason who laughed his hairy bear ass off when Viktor walked out with his new, red headed, chest accessory.

"Need a hand, old buddy?" Mason asked jogging over to him, eyes twinkling with mirth.

"Nope. Everything is just fine," Viktor said with a scowl as he stalked toward a parked, black Yukon.

"You going to introduce me to your girlfriend?"

"She's not my girlfriend," Viktor muttered through gritted teeth.

"Sure she's not, and yet, I'll bet that's the closest a woman's been to you in months."

"Are you trying to imply something?"

"Yeah, that you're a workaholic who needs to get out more."

Viktor had no retort for that. It was true. "I'm perfectly happy with my life thank you." He didn't need anything more. He owned his condo, which held a large fridge stocked with beer and meat. Possessed a gun collection large enough to take over a small state. Oh, and he had cable. What else did a croc need? Certainly not a woman to muck things up.

"You still haven't told me who the redhead is," Mason said.

"Meet Project X081. She's a little concerned about the size of the sky."

"Ha, if she thinks that's big wait until she sees the ocean."

A shudder went through her and Viktor frowned at his friend. "Shut up. Can't you see she's scared?"

Mason could have caught flies with his open mouth. He shook his head. "Scared? Since when do you give a shit? Let's go down memory lane, shall we? What did you tell me when we were parachuting into that sand lizard terrorist complex? Oh yeah, if you're going to piss your pants, put on a diaper."

A grin split Viktor's lips. "That was different."

"Different how?"

"Because it is." How, he couldn't have coherently explained. He didn't understand why he allowed the female to continue to cling to him closer than a wetsuit. Not understanding didn't mean he peeled her off though.

"Oh, wait until the guys from our unit see this." Mason danced a few feet back and a bright flash blinded Viktor. Before he could tear the camera from Mason's grasp and shove it where the sun didn't shine, Mason darted off, laughing like a maniac and waving the device.

Great. Now everyone would see him wearing a woman. On second thought, that might enhance his reputation. Everyone always did say what a cold bastard he was. His last girlfriend, a few years back, said he lacked a pulse. He didn't, it just beat very slow.

Or usually did. With a womanly shape pressed against him, his heart actually pattered a little faster than usual.

Probably from the jog up the stairs with his burden. He'd have to hit the gym more to make up for his lack of physical endurance.

Reaching the big, black truck with tinted windows, he pulled open the passenger door and saw Jessie sitting in the driver seat, tapping madly on her tablet. She didn't look up.

"Ahem."

"I'm busy," she muttered.

"I need a hand."

"Since when?" When he didn't reply, she raised her eyes from the screen. Her lips twitched as she looked him over. "Forget a hand. Don't you mean the jaws of life?"

"Not you, too."

She grinned wider. "Oh, come on. It's not every day I see you hugging someone."

"I am not hugging her. I am merely making sure she doesn't fall off."

An arched brow spoke eloquently of what she thought of his claim.

"Are you going to help me or not? She's one of the victims, obviously. We need a trauma team." Maybe some oil to loosen her grip.

"Sorry, Viktor. You just missed the last one."

"Shit." Now what?

Jessie set down her tablet and scooted over. She peered at his victim. "I don't see any obvious signs of injury. Does she need immediate medical assistance?"

He shook his head. "No. I didn't see any evidence of physical damage."

"Is she unable to communicate?"

"Oh, she can talk," he said dryly. "Even if some of what she says is crazy."

A red mop lifted and amber eyes glared at him. "I am not crazy."

"Really?" he queried. "We're outside under the big, blue sky."

She squeaked and hid her face again.

"Viktor! That was mean," Jessie chastised.

"Just proving my point. Now, are you going to help me?"

"I don't know what you expect me to do."

"Get her off me."

Jessie chewed her lower lip. "Um, excuse me, miss, would you mind getting off agent Smith and coming with me?"

No verbal response but a head shake clearly indicated no.

A shrug lifted Jessie's shoulders. "I tried. Guess you're stuck with her."

"Jessie!" he hissed.

"Viktor," she aped back with a taunting grin.

"I can't go back in and command the cleanup with her hanging around my neck like an albatross."

"Don't worry about it. Mason's already taken over. Although, at the time, when he called it in, I wondered what he meant by you ditching the job in favor of dating."

"I'm going to kill that bear," he growled.

"Get in line. My dad's already claimed first dibs. Looks like you're stuck with your new friend there for the moment. Hop in the back with your honey, and we'll get out of here."

"Aren't you still needed? We did our best to keep the computers intact so you could extract their information."

"You caught the bad guys completely by surprise. They didn't have time to wipe anything. Mason established a link to their computer and is uploading the files for me as we speak. I can't wait to dig into those and see what I can find. Since I don't need to do any fancy, high tech mumbo jumbo, we're free to go back to base.

But keep in mind, if you're going to make out in the backseat, keep the clothes on because I don't want to go blind."

Grumbling about bossy, think-they're funny swans, and no good bears, Viktor managed to slide into the back seat, his passenger not loosening her grip at all until the door slammed shut. Tentatively, she lifted her head and peeked around.

"Is this a car?" she asked.

"A truck."

"And it is going to transport us?"

"We're going to take you to processing," Jessie announced, starting the engine and putting it into gear. At the first lurch, his lady tucked back into him, and holding in a sigh, Viktor hugged her loosely.

It was going to be a long trip.

Chapter Three

Damn FUC, and damn Gregory. The latter, a loyal hyena henchman for more than a few years, obviously betrayed their plans to the former – stupid agency and the bane of the mastermind's existence – and now everything was ruined. The shifter's special ops team overran the Moreau installation with guns blazing. The staff and guards put up a valiant, if useless, fight. Thousands of dollars in research was destroyed or taken into evidence. Scientists died or threw themselves at the mercy of the invading force, the traitors.

With nowhere to escape and the enemy closing in, the mastermind did the only thing it could.

When the cage in the lab was opened, it turned big eyes, brimming with tears toward the FUC agent. The mastermind murmured, "Oh thank you. Thank you for saving me from these horrible people."

The fools bought it.

As they led the diminutive figure out to the waiting chopper along with those who could still walk, the plotting began anew, the devious cogs in the mind whirling, until a suspicious guard stared a moment too long.

Muah-ha-boo-hoo-boo-hoo. Wiping false tears, a grin threatened to burst free behind a tiny hand. So long as there was a breath to take, all was not yet lost.

The idiots didn't know who they had in their midst, which suited the plan just fine. So what if they'd taken over Moreau Island Industries and rescued all the beautifully monstrous projects hidden there? The clueless animals still didn't know who the mastermind was, who hid under their very noses. Why, they even promised to provide food, clothing and shelter. The irony was giggle worthy.

But the laughter, the evil chuckle of someone not yet defeated, needed containing. *I mustn't let them know they've caught me. In their midst, I will find a way to infiltrate their network. Discover where they've sent my lovely creations and hidden my files.*

And if lucky, get a hold of a particular bunny and her baby. Oh, and toss a bit of revenge at two bears and a swan who screwed up the brilliant plan in the first place.

I haven't given up, world. I will become the greatest predator the shifter community has ever known. All shall tremble before me. Muahahaha.

"Is something wrong?" the FUC agent asked coming alongside.

Coughing into a diminutive hand, the mastermind smiled up at the oblivious shifter. "Nothing wrong. Just something caught in my throat." The taste of near success, that was.

Chapter Four

Project eventually sat on the seat beside the one called Viktor. He pronounced it funny, with a hard emphasis on the K and T, a result of his slight accent perhaps? She liked the cadence, whatever it was, although she couldn't figure out why when he spoke, shivers tickled down her spine, nice ones. She also quite enjoyed the smell of him, spicy with an overtone of something she couldn't decipher. Whatever it was, inhaling it calmed her, but at the same time, created a strange heat.

Concentrating on him, she took stock of her situation. Despite her wishes, Viktor rescued her, taking her from the only home she knew, thrusting her into a world that frightened. And it got more intimidating the farther they travelled.

Perched beside Viktor, she kept a death grip on his arm and a claim on his body. Legs draped over his lap, her fingers digging into his forearm, she tried to take in the scenery whipping by. Dizzying green at times, square with buildings at others, signs with letters and colors! Dozens of bright and bold colors. So much had happened, so many things overwhelmed her senses, her mind threatened to shut down.

Never in her wildest imaginings could she have guessed at the big world outside the laboratory. Used to confined spaces, and ceilings which boxed her in, the glimpses of the sky, soaring so high, made her feel small and insignificant. And yet, it didn't seem to bother Viktor or the woman behind the wheel of the vehicle. Did they not fear that endless space over their heads? Apparently not. If they could handle it, so could she. She hoped.

"Any word from the field team?" her rescuer asked the cocoa skinned woman driving.

"Nope. But they're still sweeping the place. The guards that are alive are being sent to a secure facility for processing, while those that didn't survive the raid are getting DNA swabbed and fingerprinted. None seem to be the mastermind though. Actually, none of the ones questioned so far can even provide a description. It's like their minds have a blank spot where he's concerned."

"Figures," Viktor grumbled.

Project held her tongue as she listened. Despite Viktor's assurance and claim he took her to safety, she knew from experience how devious the mastermind could be. Rumors abounded, tossed around amongst the guards who didn't temper their conversations around the projects, of the retaliation meted when one of their ranks let loose their tongue in the wrong company. The mastermind didn't like those who told tales, even if none had much to say. The brains behind the operation seldom left anything to chance, even their identity. Project suspected the daily pills they were forced to swallow had a lot to do with the memory lapses of her cellmates. Everyone except for her. Project knew well the mastermind's face.

Exactly how did she recall when no one else seemed to? She theorized the 'incident' made her less susceptible, not that she ever admitted it. She played dumb like all the rest, lest the mastermind decide to terminate the lab's longest running experiment. Even now, in supposed safety, Project kept quiet about what she knew. Habit was a hard thing to break.

"So what's your name?"

A nudge from Viktor startled her.

"She's talking to you," he said.

Project glanced at Viktor, his hard gaze making her shiver. "Me? I am Project X081. But the doctors call me Project for short."

He frowned, but she didn't recoil. She'd already noticed he grimaced a lot, but it didn't mean he followed up with violence. Actually, she found him quite attractive even when he wore his grim, forbidding look.

"You're not a prisoner anymore, so you can tell us your real name. The name you had before you went to that place."

"I have no other name." Or none she remembered. Unlike the others brought in their teens and adult years, Project's memories began in a cell. Not the one they eventually found her in, but similar in almost all respects. She'd moved around a few times in her life, the voyages a fearful thing comprised of restraints and blindfolds.

"Did you have your memories erased?" Viktor asked.

She shook her head. Then nodded it. "No. Yes. Maybe. I don't know. I wouldn't exactly know would if someone did. Or didn't. It's possible."

Viktor's eyes almost crossed as he attempted to follow her logic.

"How old were you when they captured you?" asked the woman driving.

"I don't know. I can't even be sure I was captured. I think I might have been born in the laboratories. I've only ever known the labs and the dungeons they kept us locked in."

The vehicle swerved, and panicked, Project flung herself on Viktor and clung for dear life.

"Shit, Jessie. Take it easy, would you?" he grumbled.

"Sorry. I'm just a little shocked by your friend's announcement. I didn't realize the mastermind had been taking prisoners and experimenting for so long."

"You and me both," he muttered. "You don't remember going to that place, so let's try a different angle to see if we can jog your memory. How many years did you spend in their custody?"

Project shrugged. "I don't know. We don't have calendars or ways to mark time. A long time though."

"How old are you?" Viktor asked. "Eighteen? Nineteen?"

Project giggled. "Oh no. Not that young. According to Doctor Keljoy, I turned twenty six this year."

"Still so young," he remarked.

"How old are you?" she asked.

"Old enough to know better."

Not an answer, but it seemed the woman called Jessie understood the cryptic response because she laughed. "You're never too old, Viktor."

He grunted in reply. Conversation done for the moment, Project snuggled closer, and he didn't push her away. Why she found his presence comforting, she couldn't have explained. He smelled nice, that played a part. He appealed to her visually. But more inexplicably, she felt safe with him. He projected an aura of confidence and menace that should have made her flee – or wet her pants – but instead, attracted her.

Until she felt secure, or able to face the new world he'd thrust her in with some measure of competence, she'd stick close to him. Real close. She nuzzled her nose against the skin of his neck, a low rumble of pleasure rattling from her. He stiffened, and not just his upper body. A part of him under her buttocks, got harder too, it went from a firm nudge, to a thick one. Innocent in many ways, Project still knew what it meant. He found her attractive. For some reason, this elated her.

In the dungeon, most of the guards and doctor's ignored her. Mastermind's orders. Project was too valuable for them to accidentally damage. Not that she understood what made her so special. Other than her ability to resist most drugs, she was a failure in every other way.

While tall, she wasn't big and strong like some of the others held captive. She couldn't change into her animal shape, heck, she didn't even know her animal shape. She didn't possess super speed or strength, nothing. And yet, Mastermind prized her, keeping her alive even as so many others were killed after the doctors deemed them useless.

But Viktor didn't know about her special status. He'd never gotten the warning to stay away. He found her attractive regardless of her less than pristine exterior.

Despite the boring start to her day, things were looking up. She rubbed her bottom against the bulge, and snuggled closer. *Way up.*

*

Viktor suffered the strangest agony during the car ride, one of a rock hard cock and tight balls. It annoyed him. Since when did rescued waifs turn him on? It wasn't even as if his mystery lady did anything overtly sexual, other than cling to him like a leech in the Amazon. But still, something about her nearness, the heat of her, roused his sluggish, cold blood.

Sick croc. Dirty, and a victim of experimentation, he should have set her aside the moment she latched onto him. Found someone else for her to cling to as fear kept sending her for the safety of his arms. However, for some strange reason, the idea of her in someone else's grasp didn't sit well with him at all.

He blamed it on his sense of responsibility. She'd chosen him to trust and he owed it to her to get her to a place where she felt safe enough to let him go. But really, was there anywhere safer than with him? Skilled, in more ways than he could count, in methods to subdue an opponent and defend himself, she'd inadvertently chosen well when she decided to use him as her personal protector. If only she'd stop nuzzling him and making those rumbly sounds. Not one to cuddle, it appalled him to realize how much he enjoyed it.

Instead of focusing on how her warm breath tickled his skin, or her frame fit so comfortably in his arms, he thought of other things, like how she'd gotten captured at a young age. Young enough she didn't recall who she was, because he refused to contemplate the possibility she'd been born and created in a lab. Some things were just too farfetched to believe, even for him.

What kind of sicko preyed on children? Took their identity and gave them a file number. It angered him. Here was a beautiful young woman – *too young for an old croc like me* – who'd lost years of her life because of some perverse quest for power. *I will help her get revenge.* And if it involved killing, well, he was good with that. He'd not invested in all those boxes of ammunition for nothing.

The ride passed uneventfully, and Jessie parked the truck at the back of the building that housed FUC headquarters. Viktor opened the door and slid toward the opening while sexy enigma clung to him.

"We're going outside for a minute," he told her. "You might want to close your eyes for a second."

His redheaded neck-scarf clamped them tight while Jessie stifled a snort. He flicked his middle index at her mirth, but the swan, with a honk in reply, only shook harder. Eyes scanning the alley, which was clear, Viktor entered the service door and took the stairs two at a time up the several flights to the office. A man his age needed to keep in shape, so he eschewed elevators when possible for any chance at exercise. Carrying his redheaded lady provided an extra element of exertion he needed. He lied to himself instead of admitting that perhaps his decision stemmed from the fact her bare feet would find the concrete steps uncomfortable.

Once he reached the last landing, though, he halted before going through the door where everyone would see him and his new fashion accessory. Bare feet or not, if he carried her in, he'd have to kill a lot of his coworkers if they dared laugh. Besides, there was carpet just past the door, industrial low pile stuff, but still soft enough to keep her feet from harm.

"You need to let go now." Yeah, he said it, but he didn't loosen his grip right away.

Golden eyes opened and peered at him. "Is it safe?"

He snorted. "Depends on your definition. Most people would say getting this close to me is tantamount to a death wish."

"You wouldn't hurt me."

Spoken with such conviction. It warmed him. And made him scowl. "You shouldn't trust so easily. You don't know me. I could have nefarious intentions."

"Ooh, that sounds like fun."

He almost choked. "I could snap your neck before you could blink if I chose."

"But you won't." She beamed at him.

He sighed. "Just get down, would you? I don't need the entire office making fun of me."

"Sorry." She loosened her grip and slid down his body.

He enjoyed it way too much. Or a certain part of his physique did, at any rate. When she took a step away, he immediately noticed the ebbing heat.

"I'm going to take you in now to meet my boss. I don't want you to freak out, but keep in mind there's going to be some other shifters in there as well. All good guys, of course. Nobody here will hurt you."

"You wouldn't let them."

No he wouldn't. In that, she was absolutely right.

Stalking into headquarters, glaring at anyone who might dare to say a word about the woman who clung to his arm, he garnered some looks, but not as many as he feared. The woman at his side, who really needed a name, peeked around, not so much fearful as curious and cautious.

"What is this place?" she asked, returning the frank stares of the handful of other FUC agents who looked her way.

"This is FUC headquarters."

"A sex place?" She said it on a squeak.

"No," he hastened to correct. "FUC as in the Furry United Coalition. We are a group of shifters working to aid our kind against crime as well as discovery by the humans."

"Everyone here can shift?" she asked, glancing up at him with round eyes.

"Every single one."

"But there's so many." She took a sniff. "And the flavors… I never knew so many kinds existed. How marvelous you all work together."

"This is just a fraction of our population. There are shifter communities all around the world, as well as

FUC offices. We've integrated so well with society, we even work and live among the humans."

"They don't know our secret?"

"The humans? No. Although, some do suspect. Most though, treat the possibility of our existence as a joke."

"And if they were to find out?"

"Discovery would mean war, or hiding. The humans don't like anything they perceive as different, and people who can turn into animals would definitely fall under that category." He flashed her some pointed teeth, a mouthful that he knew for a fact was more copious and deadly than most people owned.

"What's your animal?" she asked.

"What does your nose tell you?"

She wrinkled it and looked so cute as she concentrated, he bit the inside of his cheek lest he do something stupid, such as kiss those soft lips. "I don't know. You kind of smell like Bob. He was an amphibian, and yet at the same time, you're nothing alike."

"You're comparing me to a frog?" He said it with disdain. "Not even close. I'm a crocodile."

"I've never seen one of those. Are you fearsome?"

His chest puffed out and the pupils of his eyes turned into vertical slits. "Very."

A smile brightened her face and her eyes shone. "I would love to see your crocodile sometime."

"Maybe, if the opportunity arises." Not likely. The chances of him encountering her after today hovered in the low to not likely range. But, he didn't tell her that. More disturbing, the thought of not seeing her again didn't sit well with him. That or he suffered indigestion. "What about you? What's your animal?" As a reptile, his sense of smell sucked, even in human form.

She shrugged. "No idea."

A crease knit his brow. "What do you mean, you don't know? Haven't you ever shifted? Or did the scientists keep you too drugged to manage it?"

"I'm pretty sure I have. I just don't remember it. It drove the scientists nuts. They'd order me to change, and I'd try, really I would, but I'm a failure. I can't even sprout a hair or a claw."

Never before had he heard of or encountered such a thing. Shifters didn't have to try to change into their animal. It just happened, like flexing a muscle. It was part of who they were. Did his senses fool him? Was she perhaps not a shifter after all, but a human victim? Only one way to find out. Viktor grabbed a coworker walking by and pulled him close. "Smell her."

"What?" Conrad, an older rat with a wicked sense of smell, recoiled.

"Sniff her and tell me what her animal is."

Conrad, casting him a wary look, leaned in and inhaled. His mystery lady didn't quite crawl up Viktor's body at the intrusion on her personal space, but it was close.

"Fox. Red fox, actually, mixed with something funky."

"Fox? A mammal then." Which made her warm blooded, and a definite no-no to his cold blooded self. While some species could mix and procreate, mammals and those belonging to the crocodylidae family couldn't. Not that he cared. He had no interest in her as a mate, even if she did fire up his sluggish pulse.

"Viktor!" Kloe's call turned his attention away from his redheaded victim whom he refused to call Project – way too demeaning.

"What?" he yelled back.

33

"Don't you 'what' me, you ornery croc. Get over here and report."

Grinning, he looked down at his wide-eyed arm ornament. "Come on. The boss wants to see us."

"Why?"

"Because she's the boss. Don't worry. She doesn't bite." *But I do.*

Slim hands latched around his arm in a grip worthy of any predator, and his recued lady bit her lower lip as he strode across the vestibule to talk with his employer.

A giraffe shifter, Kloe watched them approach, her long neck tilted in curiosity. "They told me you were bringing in a victim yourself, I just didn't believe it. I wish I'd thrown some money into the pot."

He frowned. "There's a wager going on?"

"Noooo." Kloe said it slowly, and he wanted to groan. Great, just the kind of thing he tried to avoid. And he knew who was behind it. Mason. He'd kill that bloody bear. Ignoring his obvious scowl, Kloe said, "Hello young lady, my name is Kloe, head of this FUC office."

Tucked against his side, she answered. "Hello. I'm Project."

Kloe appeared taken aback. "Oh goodness. There's no need to call yourself that anymore. You're among friends. You can use your real name once more."

"She doesn't remember her name," he supplied.

"Oh." That flustered his boss for a moment. "Well, I'm sure Jessie will find it when she has a chance to go through the files. Now, we need to figure out what to do with you. I'm afraid there were more victims than expected. We're finding ourselves short of space to house them all. Do you require immediate medical assistance?"

He nudged his rib warmer.

"I'm not hurt."

Kloe appeared relieved. "Oh good. That will make it easier to pair you up with an agent until we find more permanent accommodations. A pity Miranda is still out of town. She would have jumped all over you."

And possibly driven his rescued lady crazy with inane chatter, but at least Miranda was deadly with a weapon. Not that she needed it with her new husband, a grizzly bear who was more likely to maul first and scoff at asking questions later.

With Kloe taking her in hand, though, it meant Viktor's part was done. Time to leave. "Since you've got this, then I guess I should go." He tried to peel the bruising fingers from his arm. It didn't happen. His little red fox clamped them back on faster than he could remove them.

Kloe tried to help him. "It's okay. No need to fear, um, Project. You can come stay with me if you'd like." She held out a hand.

"No." His rescued lady shook her head wildly and tucked herself behind him, out of reach. "I'll stay with him."

"If you insist," Kloe replied, caving immediately. "Viktor, she's staying with you."

"What? No."

"Oh yes. And that's a direct order, agent."

"What are you doing?" he asked, his tone low and harsh.

A ghost of a smile on her lips, Kloe lifted her shoulders in a shrug. "She's obviously formed a bond with you. Given her trauma, it would be detrimental to try and break it without some professional help. Don't worry. I'm sure it won't be for more than a few days."

Days? Panic suffused him. "But – my work?"

Kloe patted his free arm. "Don't you worry about a thing. I think you've earned a few days off. Use that time to recharge, maybe learn a few things from our new friend here."

"But, but –" Panicked, he couldn't speak. Couldn't form the cohesive words needed to get himself away from the fox, who muddled his iron control and made his heart beat like a mammal. "I don't know how to take care of a woman."

"Easy. Feed her."

A long and thick sausage…

"Let her use the shower."

And lick her dry when done.

"Give her a place to sleep."

In my bed, cradled in my arms.

Nooooo! Panic made his mouth work as his mind – and dick – listened to his orders and tried to process them. He couldn't take the fox home. She needed someone appropriate to care for her. Someone whose cock wasn't stealing all the blood from their brain rendering them stupid and speechless. He managed to choke out a, "But you need me on the case."

"We can call if we require your expertise."

"Kloe!" He growled her name.

His boss however wasn't listening and the next thing he knew, he found himself stuffed into another SUV, his albatross wrapped around his neck, being driven home.

This is such a bad idea. His mind kept repeating that, and yet his hands, draped loosely around her back, stroked gently in an attempt to calm his red fox. As for his cock… Engorged with every ounce of blood he owned, it seemed to think bringing her home was a mighty fine idea.

*

Project could tell Viktor wasn't too happy about the circumstances, but she, however, didn't mind them. When the elegant, older woman talked about taking her away from Viktor, an icy fear shot through Project. How did she know she could put her faith in this woman? How could the delicate female, with the long neck and gangly limbs, protect Project? Mastermind was still out there. As was that big, scary sky.

Viktor had already proven himself capable of defending, or so she assumed by the hard glint in his eye, the blood she could smell on his clothes, and the weapons he carried. In this new world, filled with strangers and large spaces, Project would stick to the one person she trusted, even if it annoyed him.

The ride, while less scary this time, was a great opportunity to snuggle him again. To her delight, the same hard nudge of before rested under her bottom. It pleased her especially since she knew he wasn't happy about the order to take her home.

Inexperienced when it came to sex, Project still understood the mechanics. She'd watched it enough when the guards and doctors came down to the dungeon to have turns with the prisoners in exchange for extras like food and blankets. No one approached Project with the same offer, though, leaving her curious.

What did sex feel like? Were the gasps and groans she heard from the other cells those of pain or pleasure? She'd asked one of the scientists once to explain sex to her. He'd mentioned something about showing her instead. He'd grabbed her, placing a slobbery kiss on her lips she didn't enjoy at all. Then, she recalled nothing, waking to find herself in her cell, with no idea what happened. As for the man who'd given her a kiss, her only kiss? She never saw him again. And no one ever touched her after that unless it was for tests. Mastermind made sure of that.

It rankled because she had to wonder, did no one find her attractive? Did they sense the strangeness in her that went beyond the fact she couldn't shift? Why did no one even attempt to flirt with her?

Viktor didn't flirt, but at least a part of his body showed a definite interest. However, an impressive erection didn't mean he'd do anything about it. He seemed pretty determined to get rid of her, which didn't sit well at all. But how could she get him to change his mind?

Musings were set aside as the vehicle drove into a large area made of concrete, pillars and ducts. Dark except for the occasion fluorescent light, she found the closed in space comforting. All around, cars were parked in neat rows.

"What is this place?"

"The parking garage under my building. There's a service elevator we can take where no one will see us."

Slowing to a stop, the driver, the same man who'd sniffed her at Viktor's request, turned in his seat, and said, "Home sweet home. Have *fun* with your guest."

Project didn't understand the inflection and Viktor, a dangerous look in his eyes, grunted in reply. Her protector exited the vehicle and, with an arm around her waist, yanked her out to stand by him. Project waved goodbye to the driver who grinned and saluted her. Then she had to scurry as Viktor strode with brisk steps to an elevator. Hanging on to his arm, she hurried to keep up.

"Where are we going?"

"My condo."

"What's a condo?"

He sighed as he scrubbed his face. "It's short for condominium. A glorified apartment. It's where I live.

Where you're going to stay too, until they find you a place."

"Do you have enough room? Is it bigger than my cell?" she asked.

Despite his lingering annoyance, his lips quirked. "Much. You'll see." He tugged her into the elevator when the door slid open and ran a card along a slot. The portal whispered shut and she felt her stomach bottom out as the elevator ascended.

Up they went. She watched the numbers climb, counting silently in her head until they reached the very last floor, number thirty five. They stepped into a square area with just one door flanked by a keypad. Bending down, he untied the laces to his boots, and glanced pointedly at the slippers someone loaned her. She kicked them off, but she wasn't sure if her dirty feet were any better. Feet clad in a pair of black socks, he straightened and tapped on the small console. A beep sounded along with a click.

Viktor opened the door and gestured her in. Smiling, Project stepped into his home, and then made a grab for him as the view overwhelmed.

Thickly muscled arms circled around her body and he spoke gently. "It's okay. I guess I should have warned you that I live in the penthouse. We're pretty high up."

It wasn't the height that bothered her but the floor to ceiling windows along the back wall that gave her a dizzying view of the city with all its twinkling lights.

Still speaking softly, he attempted to calm her racing heart. "If you're worried about falling, then keep in mind that the glass you see is even better than the bullet proof stuff. You could smash a chair in to it and it wouldn't even crack. It cost me a fortune, but I wanted to make sure my home was safe."

Counting in her head, she used the familiarity of numbers to calm her stuttering fear. "It's so big," she finally muttered as she adjusted to the vast panorama. Seeing how far the horizon extended just reminded her of how little she knew of the world, and how huge it truly was.

"Big, but nice to look at. Think of the window as a living picture. It can't hurt you, but you can admire it. And look, you're still surrounded by walls and a ceiling."

Peeking up, she said wryly, "That's a pretty high ceiling."

Again, his lips quirked. "Now you're nitpicking. Come on, I'll show you the room you're staying in. You'll like it. There's only a little window and we can hide it with the curtain."

Fingers laced in hers, he led her through the open space, the soft grey fabric on the floor swallowing her feet in a luxury she'd never imagined.

Pausing, she bounced on the cushy surface. "Ooh, this is nice. What is it?"

"Carpet."

"Your office had fabric on the floor too, but it wasn't as soft as this. I wish I could have had a piece of this to cover the concrete floor of my cell."

For some reason her observation made his features tighten. "Come." He turned, and with his shoulders rigid, led her to a door at the far end of a living area – a living area adorned with couches, chairs and guns. Lots and lots of guns, and big knives. Some of the blades were longer than her arm!

Again, she stopped and gaped.

"Are those all yours?"

"Yes. I collect weapons."

Slipping her hand free from his, she walked over to a shiny specimen mounted on brackets. She ran her finger along the edge and hissed as it sliced her skin open.

Blood welled and he growled. "Be careful. That's sharp."

"So I see," she replied wryly. "What is it for? And why is your knife so big? I can't see how that would be practical for cutting food."

He chuckled. "That's because it's for fighting, not eating. It's a sword."

"Like the knights wield in the stories," she exclaimed with excitement. "How wonderful. Do you know how to use it?"

"Of course. I know how to use all the weapons in my collection."

"Why?"

"Why what?"

"Why do you have so many? And why did you learn their use? Are you afraid of the scientists too?"

"I fear no one." He growled, and his eyes shone with a fierce glow that made her tummy flutter. "The reason I have so many is because I happen to like weapons, but at the same time, I refuse to own something I don't know how to use. You never know when a skill with a dagger, a machine gun, or even a garrote is going to come in handy."

Imagine knowing how to defend oneself from harm. How she'd love to learn that skill. "Would you teach me?" she asked tracing the grip of a pistol.

"My turn to ask, why?"

She faced him and saw him regarding her intently. "Because, I think it would be nice to know how to fight. To not be frightened. Or to have someone do things to me just because they are stronger."

Pity entered his gaze, the last thing she wanted to see for some reason. She looked away. "Forget I said it. It was a silly idea."

"Not silly. Brave. It takes courage to want to fight for yourself. And if you're willing to learn, then I'll teach you."

"Truly?" With a happy sound, she flung her arms around his neck and hugged him tight, the affectionate gesture, not one she'd practiced with anyone, and yet, with him, it came so naturally. Felt so right. So *good*.

Chapter Five

For just a moment, Viktor let her hug him, the spontaneous embrace not something he could refuse. But her enthusiasm, and his pleasure at her closeness, couldn't completely eradicate the leftover emotions from her earlier request and admission.

A burning anger filled him at her wistful expression when she asked if he would teach her how to fight. Then a deep pity followed as he caught just a hint of how her captivity must have sucked. She'd languished for so long in the mastermind's prison, she didn't recall even the most basic things, things he took for granted like carpeting for swamp's sake.

Sure, he would teach her to fight. And help her overcome her fear of the sky. He'd taken on the role of teacher in the past, mostly with grunts who needed to learn the basics of survival and combat. Drawing on his knowledge, he'd train her like he trained those men. Of course, he'd never wanted to do dirty things with them, but he could use the temptation she posed as an exercise in control. He just hoped he didn't flunk.

While the knowledge she lacked about the real world bothered him, the thing that still irked him most was her lack of a real name. Since he couldn't exactly lose his mind about her treatment, in other words, kill something to calm himself – and to provide dinner – he could do something about her name. "I'll teach you how to fight if you choose a name other than Project." He blurted out a compromise before he could chew his own arm off and beat himself with it for acting soft.

"Another name? What's wrong with Project?"

"It's demeaning."

"Oh. If you say so. I'll change it if you think it's that important. But to what? How did you choose your name?"

"I didn't. My mother did, and my father, knowing what was good for him, nodded his head and agreed. She's Russian, and what she says tends to go in my house," he explained at her blank look. That just seemed to confuse her further. He sighed. "You'll understand eventually. Now as for a name, since you can't remember the one your parents gave you, let's come up with something temporary until Jessie figures out who you are."

She chewed her lip. "Like what?"

"Surely you've heard some names you've liked over the years."

A nod of her head indicated yes, but she didn't look happy nor did she volunteer any.

"What's wrong? None of them pretty enough."

"It's just…" She paused. "The names I know all belonged to guards or doctors who took care of me. Taking one of those –"

"Is a stupid, bloody idea," he groaned. He wanted to slap himself for being an idiot. "Forget I said that. You know what? How about, I recite some names and you stop me when you hear one you like."

She smiled.

"Um…" Faced with her expectant eyes, his mind went blank. Something pretty, but unique. Damn, that was harder than he thought. The most obvious names already belonged to people he knew. He focused on his rescued fox, from her tangled mop of red hair, to her bright eyes. "Annie?" As soon as he said it, he fought not to hear that stupid rainbow song as it automatically made him think of the orphaned girl his sister watched a zillion times in his youth. "No, forget that. Tammy?"

She shook her head.

"Melanie? Patricia? Amanda? Katy? Lisa?" With each shake, he scrambled for more names. A fox? What to call a hot fox? "Cherie? Renee?"

Her lips parted and her eyes brightened. "Oh, I like that last one. It seems familiar, almost."

"Then Renee it is. Okay, now that we have a name, let's finish making our way to your room. It's got its own bathroom so you can bathe and get the smell of the dungeon off your skin."

On her own, not touching him at all, which he sickly enough missed, she entered before him and stopped dead. He bumped into her, and despite the doorframe he could have used to brace himself, chose instead to steady himself with his hands on her hips, their shape more round than the shapeless gown she still wore would have led him to believe.

"What's wrong?" he asked.

"It's so big. And pretty," she whispered.

Was he in the right room? He peered over the top of her head and saw the spare room he'd decorated for when his mother or sister came to town and insisted on visiting. Done in tones of green and grey, it looked rather plain to him with only a pair of gleaming daggers over the bed.

"It's yours until you get something better." Which, given the quality of the items in the room, even if plain, could take a while. Viktor didn't skimp when it came to decorating his home. Often in the field, in less than pristine conditions, he liked his amenities at home to compensate by being over luxurious.

"Mine? Really?" She spun and smiled at him, her golden eyes alight and for a moment, he leaned forward, almost able to taste the happiness on her lips. He caught himself just in time, and instead, moved past her to open a door.

"Here's the bathroom. There's soap and shampoo in the cabinet, along with fresh towels. I don't exactly have clothes for a woman here, but I'll scrounge up a clean shirt and pants for you to wear until someone can take you shopping."

But she didn't seem to take note of his words as she wandered around touching everything; the cool marble of the vanity, the handle of the toilet which she flushed, giggling as the water swirled away.

"Yell if you need me." Leaving her to explore, and bathe, something he wouldn't allow himself to imagine, he crossed over to his own room, leaving the door slightly ajar to hear her if she called.

Stripping, he put his clothes, filthy from the mission, into the laundry hamper. His cleaning service, shifter owned and operated, wouldn't say anything about the blood or stench of gunpowder imbuing them, not with the money he paid.

Naked, he stepped into his bathroom and cranked on the water, cold, briskly so. He needed the deep chill to dampen his inappropriate ardor for Renee, victim and mystery, who out of all the people she could have chosen to trust, selected him.

It boggled the mind. Didn't she know he was a predator? He could eat her for lunch and still have room for dessert.

Mmm, a dessert of creamy flesh sweetened with womanly nectar.

Viktor groaned and banged his head on the wall. Wrong. So wrong. Sure he'd not taken a woman out in a while, but still, he and his hand took care of business daily. Why, oh why, did one foxy lady, whom he'd known for less than a day, attack his cool control?

Even with the water arctic in temperature, and her in a different room – naked under her own watery spray – his cock bobbed, aching for something he shouldn't want. His fingers curled around his shaft, tightening and stroking in a familiar rhythm that soon had his hips jerking in time.

Forget coming though, he heard a shriek, and without thinking, he dashed out of his shower and across the hall, grabbing a gun from the dresser on his way.

The impossibility of an intruder, or even danger in his home didn't penetrate his need to protect. He heard her call, and he had to answer.

*

The shower curtain pulled back with a fierce rattle and Renee whipped her head to the side to see why. She gaped. Ogled. And just about slumped to the bottom of the tub in a boneless puddle.

An extremely naked Viktor stood there, his muscled skin, so many tanned inches of it, glistening with moisture. Her eyes roved the length of him taking in the breadth of his shoulders, the tight pectorals and well defined abs. Her gaze dropped further noting the distinct v from his waist which led down to…

Cheeks heating, she whipped her startled gaze back to his face, his low growl of warning not needed. The bobbing erection was enough to remind her to mind her manners and not stare. However, the image remained burned in her mind. The sight of him also caused the strangest reaction. Heat flushed her body and her cleft throbbed.

"What's wrong?" he asked through gritted teeth.

"Nothing." Unless, he counted the fact she now possessed a burning urge to touch him. Would his skin trail smoothly under her fingertips? Was he hot or cold at the moment? Her gaze drifted down.

"Renee!"

Oops. Caught. She tried to focus on something other than his marvelous physique. Only then did she notice the gun in his hand. "Are we under attack?"

"No."

"Do you always wash your weapons in the shower?" she asked with a creased brow. Didn't metal rust when it got wet? The bars of the cells did from the tears of the prisoners who hugged them while they cried.

"No. I've got a gun because I heard you scream and thought you were in danger."

Understanding dawned and her cheeks heated further. "Um, sorry. That wasn't a cry of fear, but joy."

"You yelled because you were happy?" He didn't sound impressed.

She nodded her head.

"Am I going to shoot myself if I ask why?"

"I hope not. Blood is hard to clean."

Viktor closed his eyes and Renee could have sworn he counted to ten. "Let's try this again. Why were you screaming, Renee?"

"The water is hot." Still standing under the warm spray, she turned her face into it, luxuriating in the decadence.

"Of course it's hot. What did you expect?"

"Cold water, of course. When they hosed us off, or the few times I was allowed the use of a faculty shower, the temperature was never anything close to this. This is beautiful." She sighed as she tilted her head back enjoying the still running water.

He swallowed hard enough for her to hear. "I see. So you don't need me?"

"I don't think so."

"Have you washed your back and hair?"

Turning, she presented him her back and peered over her shoulder. "I rinsed them. Do they look clean?" She didn't understand the tightness of his jaw, or the heated look in his eyes. Was he angry that she knew so little? Or was she inadvertently using all his hot water? Too bad. She wasn't getting out yet.

"You should use the soap and shampoo to really get clean." He pointed to a corner where some miniature plastic containers sat in a row.

Holding up a little bottle, she eyed it dubiously. "How does it work?"

"You've never washed your hair before?"

She shrugged. "If we got too dirty, and the hose didn't work, they shaved it off."

A low noise, half growl, half unknown, rolled from his throat. "We're not cutting your hair. Give that to me."

Snatching the bottle, his hand briefly touched her skin – ooh, that sent a tingle through her – as he turned and positioned her facing away from him. A moment later, she felt his fingers in her hair, kneading the strands, massaging her scalp. She rose on her tiptoes, and a happy rumble poured from her.

"I think that should be good," he said in a voice gone thick.

He pushed her under the spray and white foam ran into her eyes. She screeched. "It burns! Ow! Ow! I'm blind." So much for trusting him not to hurt her.

"Don't be such a baby. It's just the soap. Close your eyes and rinse your face. It will stop in a minute."

"But it burns," she moaned, her eyes scrunched tight, prickling unpleasantly.

A rustle of movement and he was behind her in the shower. She turned blindly, seeking the safety of his chest, and met bare skin. It instantly comforted her.

"Give me a second to rinse it out." He manipulated her head under the streaming water, his fingers weaving through her hair as he murmured. "Just a little more soap left. Keep your eyes closed."

Water flowed over her face. The pain in her eyes ebbed. She allowed herself to relax and took note of their situation. Unique didn't come close to defining it. Naked, skin to skin with Viktor, a strange heat flooded her veins. A tingle hit her between the legs and it seemed only natural to cuddle closer to him, the tips of her nipples pressed against his chest. His shaft, pinned between their bodies, swelled, and there was nothing cold about it.

His hands dropped from her scalp to skim over her back, down to her waist. For a moment he held her and the heat inside her grew. She tilted her head back, not far given her height, and opened her eyes. Her lips parted when she caught his gaze. Hooded and intense, his frank stare fairly devoured her. Pinned her in place with its intensity.

He leaned toward her, and she caught her breath, waiting for him to kiss her. Wanting him to.

"I think you're clean," he said in a low voice.

Stepping out of the tub, he grabbed a towel from the hook on the wall and draped it around himself, hiding the lower part of his body. Dazed, confused, and longing for something she couldn't define, Project – *No, I'm Renee now* – numbly turned off the taps and took the towel he offered. He disappeared while she wound it around her frame.

What just happened? Or more like, what didn't?

50

He'd almost kissed her. She knew it even despite her lack of experience. *Why did he stop?*

The hardness of his erection said more than words he found her appealing. But, he walked away. And darn it, she had to find out why. Wanted to understand what she felt. And why.

Was it normal for her to want to touch him again? To crave him against her, skin to skin? To long for his lips to touch hers?

She had so many questions. So many new sensations and feelings coursing through her body and mind. Her meager knowledge of the world and people never prepared her for someone like Viktor, a man who woke her senses in heretofore unknown ways.

If only she had someone to ask. Someone to talk to. But who would answer her questions? Or even better, show her the answers?

Only one cold blooded crocodile would do. She stalked after him.

Chapter Six

Viktor paced his bedroom. He'd dressed in jeans and a t-shirt, more clothes than he usually wore at home, but he needed the fabric. Needed it like an armor to try and cover up the remembrance of how Renee's body felt pressed against his.

He'd gone dashing into the bathroom intent on saving her. Instead, he'd almost lost a battle with his body. He couldn't erase from his mind the delectable view of her pale body. Its womanly shape – heavy breasted, wide-hipped, glistening with moisture, begging for a lick. Her hair, slicked back from her face, defined her delicate features, making her seem like a water nymph. He wanted to fall to his knees in worship.

He should have known then and there to run. Run far and fast. Called for a replacement. Done anything but lay his hands on her under the guise of helping her to wash her hair. She just about purred at his touch, and he'd so easily imagined her making that noise for a completely different reason. A carnal reason.

I want to do bad things with her. Or good things, depending on the view.

The soap in her eyes and her subsequent panic snapped him out of his thrall, for a moment, or so he'd thought, until he found himself in the shower, her naked curves rubbing against him. When she tilted her head back, staring at him with mesmerizing golden eyes, he'd wanted to kiss her waiting lips. Could see in her expression she wanted him to. Wanted him to take advantage of her willingness.

I can't!

Operatives didn't screw victims. Good agents didn't let their lust get in the way of their mission, a mission that involved protecting Renee until better accommodations were located. *And my bedroom isn't that location, even though her creamy complexion would look great splayed across the silver threaded comforter on my bed.*

With a growl of annoyance, he fled her presence to his room, diving into his clothes in an attempt to forget her touch, but even there, she haunted him still. He couldn't stop picturing her. Lusting after her. It made no sense. His body, usually so cold and obedient, flushed hot, as if he'd caught a fever.

Maybe she carried a virus. Something from the lab that jumped over to him. Yeah. That made the most sense. Any excuse to deny how she made him feel. *Now if only the cure didn't involve me jumping her bones.*

He'd have to speak to the doctor about a less carnal remedy.

In the meantime, he needed distraction. Since he lacked a sparring partner, he'd have to rely on cooking, immerse himself in the preciseness of measuring and preparing a feast. Before he could make it to the kitchen, though, she appeared, wrapped in only a towel. *Fuck dinner, let's go straight to dessert.*

"Why aren't you dressed?" he snapped. Something with buckles that went neck to ankle, preferably.

"You didn't bring me the t-shirt you promised. And I couldn't put back on the dirty gown. It smells bad." She wrinkled her nose.

Instantly chagrined, he darted back to this room and grabbed the smallest shirt he could find and a pair of track pants with a drawstring. Turning around, he discovered she'd followed him.

Renee ran a hand along his comforter. "This is nice," she said. "And so big. I thought my bed was large, but this is massive."

Massive? He'd show her massive. He shook the dirty thought. "Yours is queen sized, while this is a king." Plenty of room for wrestling naked. "Here you go." He thrust the clothes at her and waited for her to leave.

"Thanks."

To his dismay – and delight – she dropped the towel, displaying once again her curvy assets. A gentleman would have looked away, but this croc found himself hypnotized by the red curls at the vee of her thighs. Thankfully, she broke the spell when she dropped his shirt over her head, its shapeless and large size covering her to mid-thigh. But the sight of her, glorious perfection, remained burned on his retinas.

She sat on the foot of his bed, but before she could pull up her legs to yank on the pants, and give him an even more interesting view, he ran away to the safety of the kitchen, his breath coming in pants as if he'd run a race. He had in a sense. A sprint to get him away from temptation.

When Renee entered a moment later, he still had his head stuck in the freezer.

"What are you doing?" she asked from behind him.

Lowering his body temperature? Probably not the right answer to give. "Looking for dinner. Do you like seafood?"

"I don't know. What is it?"

Instead of explaining, he showed her. The act of preparing the food kept his hands and eyes occupied. She perched on a stool, asking questions and making observations. He kept his answers short, clipped, trying to act like he normally would, but his stand-offish behavior didn't stop her from remarking on everything in the room.

"What's that?"

He peeked over and saw her pointing to his espresso machine. "It makes a special coffee."

"I've heard of that. What's it taste like?"

"I'll show you in the morning. I don't want the caffeine keeping you awake." No. He wanted her sleeping. In her own bed. Alone.

When he finally served them dinner, he placed her plate at one end of the dining table, and his at the other. With about eight feet of wood between them – not including the extra inches in his pants – he relaxed a little, until he choked at her next question.

"Is my body repulsive?"

A coughing fit, a drink of water and a few deep breaths later, he managed to say, "What did you say?"

"I asked if my body was repulsive. Or inadequate."

Nope. He'd heard her right. "Why would you ask that?"

"Well, while in the dungeon, I was the only one the guards never propositioned. Even the blob got some action. And then, in the shower, I thought you were going to kiss me, but you didn't."

So, she wasn't raped during her tenure. Well, that was good news. Now how to explain he found her too attractive. "You're a beautiful woman. But kissing you would be wrong."

"Why?"

"Because you're a victim."

She cocked her head and regarded him with curiosity. "But you rescued me, so I'm not anymore."

"You're still adjusting to the real world."

"Isn't sex a part of that? Or is it taboo? Are there some cultural issues I should be aware of? I know the books I read when younger talked of marriage. Is that why you wouldn't kiss me?"

Why, oh why, did he have to have this conversation? "Not everyone gets married before having sex. As for our culture, some people think intercourse is something to be shared only with someone very special. Others indulge for the pleasure of it. It depends on the person."

"What group do you belong to?"

Where was an enemy to shoot him when he needed one? "Do we need to talk about this?"

Golden eyes perused him. "Am I making you uncomfortable? I don't mean to. I just have so many questions."

"This is something you should talk about with another woman."

"But I don't know another woman. And I trust you." Her eyes suddenly widened in shock. "Is the reason you didn't kiss me because you are married to someone? Do you already have a mate?"

"No." He could see his terse reply didn't answer the question in her eyes. "I didn't kiss you because you're not only a mission, you're – you're too young." At twelve years difference, plus her naivety from her incarceration, she deserved better than old croc like him, even if he could put the younger men to shame with his strength and skill. And he didn't mean just in battle.

She puffed out her chest. "I'm twenty six. Well past the age most women discover their sexuality."

"And how would you know that?"

"Amelie said she lost her virginity at sixteen. That it's almost unheard of for women in their twenties to have never been with a man."

"And who is Amelie?"

"She used to live in the cell next to mine until they moved her to another faculty."

"Your friend was wrong. There's nothing wrong with being inexperienced at your age." By the swamp, it made her hotter.

"But I don't want to be inexperienced. Can't you teach me?"

Hell yes! Wait, no. "Renee, you can't just proposition a man like that."

"Why not? I want to learn. You said you'd teach me." There went that stubborn lip of hers, jutting out adorably again.

Despite the innocence of her demand, he couldn't help a surge of lust. "I said I'd teach you to fight not to…" Get naked and cry his name as he brought her to orgasm. "Listen, when you and your friend had this talk, did she also explain that people tend to choose someone closer to their age to be intimate with?" Dammit. Would someone please kill him now? He so didn't want to have this conversation.

"What does age have to do with it?"

"That's just how it is. If you decide to get involved with someone," over his dead, reptilian body, "then you should do so with someone young like yourself. Not old like me."

"You don't look old."

The compliment shouldn't have pleased him. But it did. He squashed his preening pleasure. "I am though. Enough of this conversation. It's not appropriate. Eat."

She stopped the questions, the oral kind at any rate, but as she ate, he caught her stares. When the meal finally ended, and he spotted her yawning, he jumped on the chance to put her to bed. Alone. Cold blooded creatures didn't snuggle. Ever.

Escorting Renee to her room, he told her a gruff goodnight before he escaped. However, even as he worked, logging onto the FUC network to check the status reports on their raid and other victims, he couldn't help his gaze from straying to the closed bedroom door.

Despite the mission, and the knowledge she latched onto him out of a sense of relief, he couldn't help wishing he'd met her under different circumstances when he was younger, less cynical, less him.

*

Renee woke feeling more refreshed than she ever recalled, the bed she'd slept in an absolute delight. To her surprise, despite the tumultuous day, she'd dropped right off, and didn't dream.

Stretching under her cocoon of blankets, she noted the golden glow creeping around the edges of the curtain. Curious, she slipped out of bed and tread on bare feet over to the covered window. She peeked around the edge of the drape, and bit her lip lest she scream and bring a panicked Viktor running. Then again, maybe she should let loose a yodel to see if he'd arrive naked again.

No. Despite how much she'd love to see his tanned flesh, she'd prefer it happen voluntarily. But before that would happen, she needed to have him change his perception of her. He was a warrior. If she wanted him to see her as something other than a victim, she needed to find her bravery, starting now, with one scary window. Despite her trembling, she forced herself to look.

Bright. Blinding. Beautiful.

The sun rose over the tops of the buildings in a brilliant array of colors that numbed the edge of her fear at the vastness of the world outside. Her first sunrise.

And it didn't send her shrieking and hiding under the blanket, or looking for a chest.

I'm making progress. Eager to share her bravery, she crept from her room and across the hall to Viktor's. On silent feet, she snuck to the edge of his bed and paused, breath held, as she allowed herself to drink in the site of him, wearing only shorts, splayed across his bed. His tanned, taut skin, so much of it, lay before her. Her lower belly tingled and for some strange reason, she had an urge to pounce and nibble on his inviting flesh.

So she did. But she no sooner landed on him than she found herself flipped onto her back, him atop her, a gun held to her head.

Shock widened his eyes. "What the hell?"

"Good morning," she said brightly.

"Do you know I could have killed you?"

"Could have, but didn't."

He sighed. "Renee, I am a trained killer. Sneaking up on me is never a good idea."

Not good for the bad guys. She knew he wouldn't hurt her. "You're fast."

"Is there a reason why you jumped on me?"

Because she wanted a nibble? Hmm. Maybe she should keep that to herself for now. She gave him the first reason instead. "I saw the sun rise."

"It scared you?"

"No. It was pretty. I thought I should tell you."

A strange expression crossed his face before his head lowered, and his forehead touched hers. "Oh, Renee. What am I going to do with you?"

A familiar nudge against her mound saw her wiggling her hips and a thrill shot through her at the rub. "I know what I'd like you to do, but you said no."

"You have no concept of boundaries." He sounded so pained.

She wondered at the cause. "Did I do something wrong?"

Rolling off of her, Viktor sat on the edge of the bed, his back to her. "No. Yes. You shouldn't go jumping in to strange men's beds."

"But you're not a stranger."

"You've known me a day."

"How many days need to pass before you're not a stranger then?"

"Renee." He said her name on a note of exasperation she knew all too well. How often did she hear it during her incarceration? '*What do you mean you can't shapeshift?*' '*Why isn't this sedative putting you out?*' '*This is not the time to do the chicken dance.*'

"What? I'm trying to learn, but really, how do you expect that to work if you're not going to answer."

"I'm not the right teacher for you."

"But I'd be such a good student." For some reason her words made him groan.

"We need to go to the office."

He changed the subject, and it worked. "We? You mean I get to go too?"

"That's usually what we means," he said. He stood and headed for his dresser to pull a shirt on. A shame. He really did look much better without it.

She clapped her hands. "Oh yay. We're going on an adventure. Wait though." Her elation burst. "Does this mean we need to go in a car again?"

"Yes."

A yummy breakfast, another hot shower and a million questions later, which Viktor answered in monosyllables, they were on their way to the FUC office.

It seemed her bravery in watching the sunrise while safely ensconced behind walls didn't extend to the reality of the outdoors and the really bright blue sky. Nor did she enjoy the chaos of driving on streets crowded with other vehicles, honking and swerving to get places. Or that was the excuse she used to justify jumping into Viktor's lap, hugging him tight and burying her face in the crook of his neck.

Whatever the true reason, she enjoyed the haven of his arms and ignored the snickers of their driver. But she smiled to herself when she caught a glimpse of Viktor flicking a digit between the seats in a very rude gesture.

Once they arrived and parked in the same alley as the day before, Viktor slipped out of the vehicle first, a hand on the butt of his gun as he searched the area. He'd explained to her on the drive over that while only their office had access to the rear entrance, and cameras guarded the place, it still paid to be cautious.

Declaring it all clear, Viktor extended his hand to her and she slid out of the car, but her toes never touched the ground. Feet clad only in the thin slippers given to her the day before, because Viktor's shoes were much too large for her, Renee held on and giggled as Viktor scooped her into his arms and jogged up the same steps as the day before.

One, two, three… She counted stairs as he climbed. As the number rose, higher and higher, her admiration of his stamina grew. *He is strong!* And not old as he claimed considering their unburdened driver, a young fellow, was huffing and puffing before they reached the halfway mark.

Entering into the FUC main area, on her own two feet, she didn't say a word as once again strangers peered at her. But with Viktor's fingers laced in hers, because she wouldn't let go, she didn't worry about anyone harming her.

A pretty blonde woman, behind a large, curved counter, looked up at their approach. "Good morning,

Viktor, and guest. Jessie's been waiting for you in the tech department. Says she might have some news on your *friend.*"

Renee frowned at the inflection and Viktor scowled. "Is Kloe in?"

"Not yet. She's visiting the victims of the lab and isn't expected for a few hours."

"Tell her I need to speak with her when she arrives."

About what, Renee wondered as he tugged her along a series of hallways until they entered a large space crammed with computers. Only a single person manned the area, and she tapped rapidly at a keyboard while lines of gibberish scrolled across her screen.

"I'm here. What have you got?" Viktor said when Jessie didn't immediately notice their arrival.

A spin of her chair and Jessie faced them. "There you are. Took you long enough. Did someone have a long night?" Jessie smirked at Viktor who growled under his breath about swans who wanted their gooses cooked. "Hey, red. Nice to see you again."

Grinning, Renee waved back.

"Mary said you had news," Viktor stated.

"I do. And I don't. Also known as good and bad."

Renee's fingers tightened around his.

"What's the bad news?" he asked.

"I couldn't find a name for her."

"I have one. Renee. Isn't it pretty? Viktor gave it to me. The name that is. Apparently, I'm too young for him to teach me about sex." Beaming, she didn't understand why her announcement made him bang his head on the wall.

Jessie choked and whirled away from them, shoulders hunched and shaking.

"Is she alright?" Renee whispered. In the cells, when someone shook, it usually meant something bad was about to happen. Or gross. It would suck to lose her clean state to projectile vomit, or worse.

"She is fine for the moment, but I can't vouch for her state later," he growled. "What other bad news do you have?"

Her voice still somewhat choked, Jessie answered. "Renee is definitely twenty six years old according to her medical file, and if they can be believed, she's been in their custody for fourteen years."

"Longest living specimen. Yay for me." Renee fist pumped like she'd seen the scientists do when they accomplished something. It didn't take the stunned look from Viktor's face.

"Fourteen years? How could we not have known this was going on?"

Jessie shrugged. "The mastermind only snowballed the research and kidnapping in recent years. Before that it was just a shifter here or there. According to the files I've recovered, all their victims, except for the ones we rescued, died at some point, usually within the first year or so. Renee's the only one who survived all the tests."

"I also survived the drugs. Lots of drugs. Some of them were quite nice, like the one that made me see everything in rainbows." She'd also liked the one that made her think she could fly until she woke up with a broken nose.

"I'm going to kill something." Viktor slammed his fist into a wall, leaving an impressive dent. Apparently not pleased with his impromptu remodel of the room, he hit it again and again.

"Why is he so mad?" Renee asked Jessie.

"He's not angry. He's expressing himself in a physical manner which is really out of character." Jessie just about shouted the last bit.

A deep breath, shoulders straightened, Viktor left the wall alone and faced them. "Sorry. My hand had an itch."

"Doesn't scratching work better?"

"Just forget I did that. Any more bad news?"

"Not really. The next tidbit I discovered, which could be considered good, is she has an immunity to most drugs, even basic anesthetics, ever since something referred to as the incident."

"What incident?" he snapped.

"I don't know," Jessie said, waving some sheets at him. "I haven't managed to decode that part of the database yet."

Two sets of eyes swiveled her way, the question clear. Renee sighed. "It's not that big of a deal. I accidentally fell in a vat of radioactive waste."

"You did what?"

"Fell. I was clumsy in my youth, and bored. I thought I'd play tag with the doctor and slipped my restraints. I was winning, too, until I fell in." Not one of her best moments.

Viktor looked about to explode and Jessie put a hand on his arm which Renee didn't like at all. She turned sideways, her hair prickled and she growled softly.

Jessie removed her hand and tucked it in her lap. "What happened after?"

"They pulled me out, but not before I swallowed a ton of it. I was sick for weeks. My hair fell out. I lost all my teeth, which thankfully grew back. Shed a bit of skin. It was not a pretty time for me. But, on the upside, when I got better, my acne cleared up and never returned, oh and almost none of their drugs worked, especially the sedatives, which drove them completely mental."

"Is that why you can't shapeshift?" Viktor asked.

A shrug lifted her shoulders. "Maybe. But I don't remember shifting even before the accident so maybe I was just defective from birth."

She didn't think with him glowering that now was the time to tell him she didn't remember much of anything before the incident. One day, she just woke in the lab. Project X081, no mother, no father, no friends. The mastermind claimed to have created her. *I made you, therefore I own you,'* the diminutive figure claimed on more than one occasion.

The only thing Renee never understood was, if they'd made her, then where did the dreams come from? The dreams where she ran on four legs through the forest. The dreams of a woman with brassy hair and a big voice who held out her arms to catch her. The cake topped with candles that wavered before her as someone sang a song. If they'd made her in a bottle, grown her in a vat, then how could she see these things? Know of them?

Scared they would take her dreams away, she told no one. And even now, as Viktor and Jessie spoke in quiet tones of other discoveries made on the lab's computers, Renee held her tongue. She feared losing her bits of fantasy. Her wishful dream that the images meant something, meant she had a family and wasn't just a project, a shapeshifting Frankenstein as the doctor's so jokingly called her. *Maybe there's someone out there who already loves me.*

Chapter Seven

Viktor kept an eye on Renee as she grew bored of the discussion and actually let go of him to wander around the room. The anger at hearing how long the mastermind victimized her wouldn't die down. He wanted to kill something. Lots of things. He wanted to shake Renee and ask her how she could act so blasé about the situation. Joking about the drugs she took. Blaming her clumsiness for falling into a radioactive vat. Did she not take any of this seriously? How could she not burn with rage for what was done to her?

He did. And he'd help her get revenge.

"Vi-i-c-t-t-o-r-r! Where are you? I'm coming to find you, Victor! You can't hide from me." The exuberant exclamations hit him a second before Renee slammed into his back, her arms wrapping around his waist tight as an anaconda. He didn't blame her. Knowing who arrived, he wanted to hide too.

His former partner, a bouncy bunny who drove everyone nuts, but who kicked ass in the field, hopped into the room and tackled him for a hug. "Victor!" Miranda shrieked. "I missed you!"

"I thought you were in the boonies, staying out of sight," he said, suffering through the embrace. Damned woodland creatures were so touchy feely. And his fox didn't like it either, judging by the growl against his spine.

"I had to come back. Doctor's appointment. And we needed more carrot cake. The local bakery doesn't make it, which is dumb because junior really likes it and they would totally make a fortune off me," Miranda said patting her rounded, pregnant belly.

"Where's Chase?"

"Miranda!" The familiar bellow of her mate made his bunny partner roll her eyes.

"In Jessie's office, honey bear," she hollered. "I'm talking to Victor."

And as usual, she mispronounced his name. His name was Viktor, not the softer American version of Victor. But he'd given up years ago trying to get her to enunciate it correctly.

While Miranda peeked to his left, then right, trying to catch a glimpse of Renee, who refused to lift her head from hiding, Chase lumbered into the room. A grizzly bear, not just as an animal, but also in nature, he scowled at everyone but his mate.

"Would you stop hopping away from me? How am I supposed to protect your furry ass if you won't stay still?"

"I told you the elevator wasn't as fast." Miranda smirked. Chase growled, and Viktor sighed. He'd gotten use to the quiet with Miranda on sabbatical. A forced vacation actually, given she wanted to work the mastermind case, but due to the fact the psycho really wanted to get his grubby hands on the sabertooth bunny and her unborn child, they'd deemed it safer to put her under guard. With her mate, father in law, and even tougher mother in law watching over Miranda, only a madman would attempt anything.

Okay, the mastermind, being nuts actually had tried to kidnap her, but they'd foiled the attempt. FUC agents prevailed and Miranda, the baby and everyone else was safe – so long as no one laid a hand on her carrot cake.

"You should have stayed in your safe house," Viktor admonished.

Miranda rolled her eyes. "Oh, pl-l-l-e-a-s-s-e." She drew out the word dramatically. "Have you ever been cooped up with three bears in a house with no honey or carrot cake?"

"She got bored," Chase remarked dryly. "Personally, I found all the sleep refreshing."

"See what I've had to put up with?" Miranda lowered her voice to a conspiratorial tone. "Did you know bears can sleep like sixteen hours a day? It's insane. I only need a good five or six."

"Because you're a spaz," Jessie remarked.

Miranda stuck her tongue out at the swan who honked with laughter.

"Hey, who threw a party and didn't invite me?" Mason loomed in the doorway with a big grin. He slapped his brother, Chase, on the back, a hard whack that didn't budge the big man. "Ha. I knew Miranda wouldn't last a week in the safe house. You owe me twenty bucks."

"Stupid agents in charge should have brought more food. Pregnant bunnies are bottomless pits apparently." Grumbling, Chase dug into his pocket and grudgingly handed over a crumpled bill.

"You wagered on me?" Miranda asked, hands on her hips.

"Yup."

"Awesome. Next time let me know though, and I'll rig it so you win, honey bear." Miranda winked as she bounced on the balls of her feet.

"Who says I lost? A nosy mother and paper thin walls," Chase added when Viktor raised a brow at his odd statement.

"Ack! Too much information. I feel sick," Mason moaned. "No fair. I just had breakfast, too."

A rough jab to the ribs and Mason shut up. Chase smiled smugly.

"Why is your friend hiding? I want to meet her." Miranda still bobbed for a peek, but Renee, overwhelmed at all the new people, didn't move from her spot behind him.

"She's kind of shy," Viktor replied, certain the entire outline of Renee's face would forever mark his back, she pressed so hard.

"Shy?" Miranda blinked and her nose twitched. "But it's me. Didn't you tell her about me? I'm hurt," Miranda exclaimed, clasping a hand to her chest dramatically. "I thought I meant something to you."

Sharp nails dug into his waist and Viktor fought not to wince. He patted the hand that currently left a bruise. "Renee, this is Miranda, my partner." The claws pressed harder. "Work partner. She's on maternity leave with her husband, Chase."

The pressure eased. Slowly, Renee peeked around his arm. "She's an agent?"

"One of the best," Miranda boasted. "When I unleash my bunny, everybody runs."

A giggle escaped his fox. "You're a rabbit? As in long floppy ears and fluffy tail?"

"Don't let my awesome exterior fool you. Inside, I am a deadly predator."

"With great big fangs. We know," Mason interrupted. "Attention hog."

"I am not!"

"Don't start," Chase growled.

His admonition didn't stop Miranda from flicking a finger at Mason, who blew her a raspberry before facing Renee, who watched them sparring with wide eyes.

"Hello there, my name is Mason. I'm also a FUC agent, and that techno geek hottie over there is my chocolate dipped delight. You might remember me from yesterday. I was part of the team that helped free you." Mason stuck out his hand, and Renee looked at it, but didn't touch it.

"You're supposed to shake it," Viktor muttered under his breath.

Slipping her hand free from his waist, Renee clasped the extended appendage and pumped it vigorously before dropping it like a hot potato.

"Nice grip. You're a lucky man, Viktor." Mason winked. Miranda and Jessie giggled. Even Chase looked amused. Viktor, however, wanted to punch his unit buddy for the remark. How dare he think of Renee in a sexual manner? *And just how good is her grip?* Damn the bear for putting the question in his head, and worse the image of how he could find out.

Maybe he'd take the nosy mammal to the training gym later on and show him why you didn't throw verbal sticks at ornery – horny – crocs.

Despite his annoyance at Mason's crude innuendo, it did have a benefit. More of Renee emerged from hiding, still glued to his side, but at least she didn't cower behind, using him as a shield.

"Oh, aren't you just the cutest thing," Miranda exclaimed. "But the clothes have got to go. Oversized men's wear is for home use only. A pretty girl like you needs color and skin tight stuff to show off your curves. Victor, you need to take her shopping."

"I don't have time. I've got some reports to write. People to talk to. You know. Work stuff." Hell, he'd even go to a dentist and freak them out with his numerous, pointy teeth, anything to avoid a trip to a store. An avid internet shopper, he bought everything online and paid for delivery.

"Then I'll take her."

"No!" Both he and Renee shouted it at the same time, which caused another round of knowing smiles he didn't appreciate.

"I stay with him," Renee explained, wrapping her arms around his waist and locking her fingers together.

"It's my job to protect her," he added, knowing it sound lame the moment it left his mouth.

"Sure it is," Miranda said rolling her eyes. "In that case, you'd better get the office to send the paperwork home, because this might take a few hours."

Hours? No. They wouldn't. He was a decorated military man. An agent with innumerable skills. But the pregnant bunny with a one-track mind didn't care.

Unwilling, and yet unable to leave Renee's side – and ordered by his boss with a snicker – Viktor got roped into going shopping. For clothes. Worst mission ever.

*

Renee could tell Viktor didn't care for the turn of events. But it wasn't her fault. The crazy blonde insisted she needed proper clothes, and truthfully, Renee wanted some too. Something pretty like the other women wore. Something to make Viktor's eyes look at her with the same warm light Chase and Mason's did when they glanced at their mates.

His boss Kloe, when Viktor reached her by phone in a desperate attempt to forestall the expedition, said nothing needed his immediate attention and when he still begged for an excuse, ordered him to go. Penned in by bears, a slightly lunatic pregnant lady, a smirking Jessie, oh, and one scowling croc, Renee ended up piling into a large vehicle with tinted windows, a minivan, Mason announced when she eyed it. Even though it had enough seating, Renee still preferred her spot in Viktor's lap, which for some reason had Miranda laughing so hard tears ran down her cheeks.

At least Renee no longer wanted to scalp the perky bunny – even if she overheard Chase mention that rabbits made the best muffs, a discussion Mason disagreed with claiming swans down was a better place to lay his head. Not understanding the conversation, or the laughter, she nevertheless relaxed and dropped her plan to maim because when she'd first seen Miranda enter, and toss herself at Viktor, she'd seen red. It didn't help the woman kept mispronouncing his name with a familiarity that made Renee grind her teeth. The fact the bunny turned out mated and harmless – if you didn't mind your teeth aching from her sugary personality – eased Renee, but not enough to want to go somewhere alone with the woman. Loud, bouncy bunny, grizzly bear of a husband or not to accompany them, Renee trusted only Viktor to keep her safe, because as she well knew, the mastermind was still out there.

A part of her wondered if she should speak up and tell them the little she knew. But really what could she add to their repertoire of information that they didn't already know. It wasn't as if she was privy to the mastermind's secret plots. Renee didn't know where the mastermind fled. She really knew nothing at all other than the unforgettable face of evil and bad acne.

She kept silent as they drove to a place Miranda called a mall, listening to the banter between the couples, Jessie having elected to join them for a lunch break while her computer decoded more of the information downloaded from the lab.

When Viktor quietly mentioned her phobia of the open sky, Chase, with a nod, drove into a covered parking area with a sea of cars. They piled out of the vehicle and Renee held Viktor's hand as they entered the shopping place, trying to walk without looking like a fool in the flip flops Miranda gave her to wear. Apparently, slippers weren't meant for public places. Viktor groaned when Miranda added shoes to their shopping list.

The vast amount of people moving in the mall gave her a miniature panic attack and Renee tucked herself under Viktor's arm. Her heart rate quickened as her eyes scanned the many faces. Did the mastermind hide among them? Minions? Did the people all look at her, knowing she was different?

"No one will hurt you," Viktor murmured.

She peeked up at him. "But there's so many. How can you be sure?"

Miranda snorted. "Oh please, if I wasn't pregnant, I could take these humans on by myself. With a little help, Victor could too."

"Gee, thanks for the vote of confidence," he replied dryly. "But seriously, even the mastermind would hesitate before acting in front of the humans. We've all got a vested interest in keeping our shifter identity secret. And if I'm wrong, that's what my Magnum is for."

"You've got a Magnum?" Mason said. "Nice. I just brought my Browning."

"Freaks," Jessie muttered. "A good Taser is all you need."

"Knives are better," Miranda added.

When everyone looked at Chase, he shrugged. "I'm old fashioned. I prefer to use my fists."

Renee blinked at their casual discussion of weapons and implied violence. They were all crazy. Just her kind of people.

Easing out from Viktor's arm, she threw her shoulders back, kept a firm grip on his hand, and followed as Miranda and Jessie taught her how to shop.

Or as Mason called it, making a credit card scream. She'd never had so much fun in her life.

As they browsed racks of clothes, the vibrant colors jumping out at her, Miranda babbled. Aimlessly, or so it seemed initially.

"So, you and my partner. What's up with that?"

"Excuse me?" Renee asked not grasping the question.

Jessie rolled her eyes. "What Miranda is trying to say is, are you and Viktor an item? You know, dating?"

"Or boinking. Lots of relationships start out that way," Miranda added sagely, a wisdom marred only by the smirk on her lips.

"Viktor is guarding me until Kloe can find me a home."

"How romantic," Miranda sighed. "It sounds kind of like how I ended up with Chase. Except, I was his uber killer bunny, and he was a grumpy ol' bear. I saved his butt. He mauled some minions to save mine. Some carrot cake and awesome sex later, we were mated and in love."

"And screwing everywhere," Jessie added with a snort. "It's how she got knocked up so quickly."

"Knocked up?" Renee's nose wrinkled at the expression.

"Pregnant."

"Oh." Renee peeked at Jessie. "And how did you and Mason end up as mates?"

"Um, we were kind of working a case together and my, um, dad forced him to marry me."

"So you're not happy?" Renee asked, puzzled because she'd seen the intimate and heated looks between Jessie and her bear.

"Oh, we're in love and all that jazz. I'm just not as vocal about it."

"Liar!" Mason yelled from across the store where he apparently eavesdropped. "She's a screamer."

Jessie glared.

"And violent too," he added. "Love you." His sheepish grin did nothing to erase his mate's glare.

"He is a dead bear," Jessie growled.

A giggle escaped Miranda. "You sound just like Chase when you say it like that." She sobered. "But seriously, Renee, if you're interested in Viktor, don't let his grouchy nature keep you away. A man like him is worth the trouble."

Finally, someone who could answer some of her questions. "How do I know if I'm interested?" she asked, casting a glance at Viktor who stood at the opening of the store, arms crossed, scowling. Despite his fierce demeanor, she noted the women who cast him appraising glances. She didn't like it one bit.

"Judging by the way you're staring deadly daggers at the ladies checking him out, I'd say you're interested."

"But he's not," she replied, shoulders slumping. "He thinks I'm too young."

Jessie snorted. "He might be saying that to help himself keep his hands off of you, but trust me, he's interested. If he wasn't, not only would he already have found you a place to stay, he wouldn't have come shopping."

"He came to keep me safe."

Miranda and Jessie shared a look before bursting into gales of laughter.

"What's so funny?" Renee asked.

"You are with me, Mason and Chase. Between the three of us, even with me pregnant, we could keep off a small army. Add in Jessie with her tech skills and we could take over this mall."

"Forget just the mall," Jessie huffed. "We'd own this city."

"So he came because he likes me?" The very idea elated Renee and she glanced over again to find his eyes on her. She smiled, and ignored the nudges as he returned it, a light lipped version, but still, for her.

But how to get him to see her as more than a charge – and past her age? "What should I do?"

"Jump him," Miranda volunteered.

"I did that this morning and he almost shot me."

Jessie coughed. "Um, not literally. She meant, seduce him."

Hands on her hips, Miranda shook her head. "No. I meant jump on his bone. I like to get a little distance before I do a running leap. Oh, and it works best naked."

"Pervert."

"I wouldn't talk, swan. I hear Mason had to replace his cuffs. I wonder why?"

A ruddy color brightened Jessie's cheeks.

Renee watched the byplay with fascination. She didn't quite grasp all of it, but she stored it for later use. Use with Viktor.

"Normal people," Jessie said, turning her back to the blonde bunny, "Don't usually try to tackle their love interest to the ground. They kiss first. And then let things go from there."

"Kiss. Gotcha."

"And grope," Miranda added. "They like that."

Jessie nodded in agreement.

The conversation on how to seduce ended at that point as Viktor approached. Snickering, Mason and Chase closed in too, but they wouldn't tell their friend what they found so funny. A relief to Renee, because despite all the advice, she didn't know if she had the courage to take the first step.

But if she didn't, would she regret it for the rest of her life?

Chapter Eight

Elsewhere…

The mastermind played dumb in the corner while the doctors talked. It went against the grain to melt into the background. Years of calling the shots was hard to stifle. But care was needed with the next level of plotting and deviousness. It wouldn't do to get caught, not now, not when the enemy held all the cards.

The safe house they'd taken all the least damaged prisoners too – including one wily plotter – wasn't exactly the heart of FUC. A nondescript building, converted into a temporary hospital, it teemed with agents and guards determined to keep the prisoners safe. The irony that they also inadvertently protected their greatest threat was almost too delicious to bear. Not so entertaining was getting out of the safe house without causing suspicion. That proved harder than expected.

Because the agency feared the mastermind coming after the failed creations, they guarded the place better than the White House. And yes, the mastermind knew about that first hand. Damn the secret service for foiling the plot to change the president into a shifter!

However, while escape didn't lie in the cards, other things, interesting things were still happening. For example, the doctor – Nolan Manners, aged thirty one, an almost pure blooded male from one of the larger feline breeds – made an interesting discovery about the experiments, something all the other scientists, employed over the years by the mastermind, missed.

A solution so simple. So divine. Well within the reach of a small creature who, as usual, went unnoticed. But sitting in the shadows wouldn't achieve the goal of transformation.

"Can I help?" the mastermind asked in a squeak. Would the idiot in charge fall for the smallest ploy in the world? Underestimating.

The doctor's gaze peered around, aiming too high, as usual. A wave of the hand on tiptoes and Dr. Manners looked lower. Then frowned.

"Help with what?"

"I know what the mastermind was doing with the experi – er victims. Appalling."

"Aren't you a victim, too?"

Oops. "Yes. Yes, of course I am, but once they did this to me…" A sweep of a hand towards a long hated, diminutive figure, and the suspicion in the doctor's eyes eased. How easily they were fooled. "…they didn't bother with me after."

"We'll do our best to reverse the conditions and bring you back to your regular state. But it will take time, research and tests, tests best done by qualified personnel. Thanks for the offer to help, though."

And that quickly, the doctor dismissed the offer. Relegated the mastermind, smartest creature ever, to a non-status.

Unacceptable.

It was grade school all over again. Always acting as if size and appearance were all that counted. How those years still burned. The humiliation still fresh, even after all this time. Hide the smallest creature's lunch bag. Laugh while they hunted for it. Those who thought themselves so cool paid for their jest, going home with their faces green and pants heavy because small didn't mean stupid, and the ingredients for screaming diarrhea lurked everywhere.

Things should have changed with age. Gotten better. However, despite all the money, and power, people still laughed. Didn't respect the large brain hidden in the small body.

If only the formulas would work. If only the scientists could have figured out how to replicate X081's condition. If only they could have gotten a sample of that stupid saber toothed bunny's DNA. Damn, that FUC agent and all her friends.

Most of all though, if only they'd kidnapped the right doctor, a doctor who looked at the data with more than the knowledge he'd learned by rote, who cast a fresh perspective on an old problem. A doctor like Nolan Manners.

Eyes narrowed behind thick lenses, the mastermind watched the doctor as he wrote on his whiteboard, showing his assistant the problem with the genetic code in the lovely experiments. Saw as he highlighted the switch to turn the experiments back to their previous physical state. Or even better, if the switch was reversed, turn them in to a more evolved one.

The final answer in a lifelong dilemma. At last, physical size and deadly power could belong to the mastermind.

Muah-ha-ha-ha. Oops, figured the laughter would slip out with just the right cadence at the wrong time. When eyes turned to peer with suspicion, a shrug of small shoulders and a lame, "I'm just so happy you've found a solution," appeased them.

Fools.

Chapter Nine

A tomato sauce simmered on the stove. The bread, slathered in garlic butter, toasted in the oven. The grated cheese overflowed in a bowl while Renee lounged on the couch watching Viktor's favorite cult movie – Rogue, a violent flick about a man eating crocodile, based on the life story of his uncle Jack. Maybe not the best movie for a recovering victim, but, he'd put it on in the hopes of defusing the silly – gratifying – crush she seemed to have developed for him. He wasn't stupid. How could he miss the way she clung to him? The way she watched him? Snuggled him? And worse, he wasn't the only one to see it.

His friends ribbed him about Renee, good natured taunts urging him to go for it. But he couldn't. Shouldn't. She needed to see the world. Live a little before she could know what she truly wanted. Who she wanted. Problem was, once she got a taste of what life could offer, she'd soon forget her interest in an ornery old croc, which was for the best. He didn't need some timid fox hanging off him at every turn. Nor did he need the trouble of caring for someone else full time.

As Renee gasped and oohed at the various action sequences, Viktor puttered around the kitchen, alone, prepping dinner. Time to drain the pasta before it went past its al dente stage. Despite his attention to the task – and his resolve to stay away – his eyes kept flicking over to her, watching as she leaned forward at the intense parts. Lips quirking when she jumped at the scary – for her – scenes. A part of him wanted to join her and indulge in some relax time. He didn't. He'd finally peeled her off. Convinced her, well, more like she decided, that she didn't need to hang on to him at every turn. At least not inside the condo. A great step forward for her. He should have celebrated, instead, sick croc that he was, he missed the feel of her pressed against him. Watching her just wasn't the same as wearing her.

Nothing about her resembled anything he'd ever encountered.

A prime example? Shopping with her should have gone to the top of his list of things to never do again. It didn't. Instead, spending his money – because he bloody well insisted, knowing how cheap FUC could be – topped the list of most painful thing ever. Even worse than the time he spent in the desert, silver poisoned and parched. Seriously. He spent the afternoon in agony, tortured by the delightful curving of lips he couldn't kiss. Suffered the fist clenching misery of seeing other men admire the curves he possessively thought of as his. Went tight jawed with the blue balled pain of helping her zip up, his hands skimming across the smooth skin of her back because even in the change rooms, he hovered nearby – to protect of course. And then, there was the mind muddling blur of a ride home where she sat on his lap, her new short skirt riding up, her bottom grinding and bouncing on his lap as she conversed animatedly with the others.

Was it wrong of him top fantasize how he'd like to slide his hand up her thigh and see which of the decadent lace confections she chose to wear?

Worse, he could see the knowing smiles on his friend's faces, smirks and jests which Renee thankfully didn't notice. As they dropped him and Renee off, Mason pulled him aside and with a nerve he wouldn't long possess – not once Viktor got done with him – reminded

Viktor, who'd bloody well trained him, to wear a skin on his lizard if he was going fox hunting.

Before he could retort, the gang left, leaving him alone with a victim, who looked like a delectable vixen in her new duds. A red haired temptation he wanted to wear on his…

"Supper," he snapped, slapping the plates on the table. Startled, she jumped, and tumbled to the floor in a splay of limbs that answered one question at least. Pink lace.

Scrambling to her feet, Renee made her way to the table and slid her plate over so she could keep watching the movie.

Annoyed for some reason that she chose to concentrate on the screen instead of him, Viktor attacked his food. He speared the meatballs. Violently twirled the spaghetti onto his fork. Whipped the salad into his mouth. Chomped the bread into bits.

So intently did he demolish his food, it took him a moment to realize she stared at him. Caught mid forkful, he sucked the noodle in with a wet slurp.

"Are you mad?" she asked.

"No." Couldn't she see he was ecstatic? His plan to get her to realize he wasn't the best thing since chocolate cake was working. Dammit.

"You look mad."

"Don't I always?" he replied sarcastically.

"No. Usually, you're smiling at me. Or frowning. But not mad. Is something wrong?"

Did the fact he wanted her on the table, legs spread, panties shucked, primed for his version of dessert count? No, he better not mention that. She'd probably climb right onto the tabletop and give him what he wanted. Thank God she couldn't see his hidden crotch, because he currently sported an erection that would have fed her easily with plenty left over. "I'm not mad. Just hungry." Very hungry for a taste of a fox.

"You didn't eat enough at lunch, which, by the way, was really yummy," she said, waving her fork at him.

How could he eat when she groaned her way through her first Big Mac? It was all he could do to stay upright.

He changed the subject. "You did really well today. I was proud of how you comported yourself with the crowds."

She grinned. "I did do good, but only because I knew you wouldn't let anything happen to me. But just so we're clear, I still don't trust that sky." She scowled. "It's too big and open. The city really should think about putting a roof over it."

The chuckle slipped from him before he could stop it. "Yeah, I don't think that's going to happen. Give it more time." An eternity if she liked, because despite the laughter of his friends and what he knew was right, he didn't mind at all the way she scurried into his lap or arms at the sight of the bright, blue sky. *I wonder if I painted one on the ceiling in here if it would have the same effect*

Sick. He was so sick. Probably because he needed some action – between the sheets and sweaty. No. Physical exertion – pumping up and down on top of her. Dammit. He needed some fucking fresh air and a swamp swim.

But how could he get away to his cabin in the woods, a cabin that was only a few hundred yards from a bog he frequented? *I could bring her with me.* Under what guise? His condo was safer. He needed to stay in touch with the office. But maybe a quiet trek into the woods would help Renee. Maybe she'd get in touch with her roots, her beast. Aha.

"What do you say we take a drive tomorrow and stay at my cabin?"

"A trip? Just you and me?"

He nodded. Then almost changed his mind at the wide smile that spread across her face. Shoot. He was supposed to be distancing himself from her. So far, his plan seemed to be failing. Funny how it didn't bother him as much as it should.

"I'd like that. What should I pack?"

He didn't utter his first reply of *nothing*. He couldn't say anything at all actually as she jumped out of her seat and flew at him. Hugging him tight, giddy with excitement, it was all he could do to keep his hands off her.

And like an idiot, I'm taking her somewhere we can be alone, and naked. Because while in the boonies, he intended to get her to try and shift. Or so he told himself because certainly a devious croc of his age wouldn't use any excuse to get a hot fox in the buff?

Chapter Ten

Skipping alongside maman, she admired, in the storefront window, her new sophisticated haircut. A short red bob that framed her face and gave her a mature appearance, unlike the wild curls of before. She looked so grown up, grown up enough, that when they went to the restaurant, she waved at her mother to sit while she went to the restroom. At twelve years old, she didn't need her maman to watch over her as she peed and washed her hands.

It wasn't until she exited the washroom that her noise twitched and the hairs on her body rose in warning. What was that smell? She knew it, yet didn't. A shifter, no make that two shifters, had recently passed by. Not recognizing the scent, she thought nothing of it until a hand clapped over her mouth and a voice hissed, "Shh. Be quiet or else."

As if. She fought like a rabid fox against her captor, not that it stopped him from dragging her to the door marked 'Reserve Aux Employés'. When the portal swung open to reveal a scummy alley, panic truly shook her. Fight!

She bit the hand covering her mouth and when he released her with a curse, she let out a shriek to beat all shrieks.

"Maman! A moi! Au sec–" She didn't get to finish as the bad man caught her again, slinging her over his shoulder in a violent heave that forced the air out of her lungs and left her gasping for breath.

She heard the rumble of a car just as her mother came screeching to the rescue.

"Mon bébé! Appelez la police. Il a ma petite." Her mother screamed for help while whacking the man who held her. He grunted, but didn't release her, and the next thing she knew, her mother slumped to the ground, eyes closed, as blood seeped from her temple.

Tossed into an open trunk, she scrambled to escape only to feel the prick of a syringe entering her arm. As her eyes grew heavy and an unnatural urge to slumber gripped her, she listened as the lid to the trunk slammed shut. It muffled the sound outside but she still heard the English speaking shifters talking, and what do you know, her mother was right, being bilingual did have its advantages because she understood every scary word.

"Are we taking the girl's mother too?"

"No," replied a high pitched voice. "The child will be easier to brain wash if she has no reminders of her past life."

"If you say so boss." A strident alarm grew louder. "I hear sirens. We'd better leave."

"To the lab!" squeaked the other. "And to success. Mua-Mua-Mua-erg. Damn these puny vocal cords."

Tears rolled down her cheeks as she sobbed quietly. *Maman, aide moi. Maman…*

Something shook her and she thrashed, crying and hitting, escaping that bad man who took her from…

"Renee! Wake up. You're having a nightmare."

Slowly, her mind foggy as the dream took its time leaving, she woke to realize Viktor held her, concern etched on his face.

"What happened?" he asked softly, pulling her to sit more fully in his lap, his cool skin lowering the temperature of her feverish one.

She raised her hand and wiped cheeks wet with tears. "I think I dreamt of my abduction. And my mother." *I have a mother!* The knowledge brought her a peace and joy she'd not realized she lacked. It seemed the idea the scientist created her in a vat of goo bothered her more than she'd thought.

"Did you remember who you are?"

Her brief elation melted. "No."

"Oh, Renee." Viktor sighed her name, then said nothing, just held and rocked her as the trembles in her frame eased.

"Je parle français," she said when her heart finally slowed down.

"What?"

The terror of her nightmare eased, the thrill of her memory returned. "I said I speak French. How cool is that? Do you think I'm from France? Do you think my mother might still be alive? How would we find her? Should I find her? What if I don't like her? What if she doesn't like me?"

"Slow down. First off, there's a lot of countries that have French as a language. And given how long ago you disappeared, and the fact we only got the paper records into the FUC computer system recently, it won't be that easy."

"Oh." She deflated again. "I guess it was silly of me to hope."

"Hey. Don't give up." He tilted her chin. "If you have family out there, we'll find them. It might take a few weeks, or months, but I'll get the FUC team on it right away."

"You'd do that for me?"

"Yes." The pad of his thumb, rough like sandpaper, yet welcome, rubbed the tears still staining her cheeks. "Don't cry. I don't like it."

"Why not?"

"Because it makes me want to hurt things, but I can't fight a memory."

"Why would you want to? It's not your problem. I'm just a mission," she sassed, throwing his words at him. She didn't take offence, not with the knowledge she possessed from Miranda that everything Viktor had done thus far for her was completely out of character, which meant he did it because he wanted to, *for me*.

"My mission is to keep you safe."

"So you would protect me from my own nightmares?"

"I would erase them if I could."

"I thought you'd never say that." She leaned in and pressed her mouth against his.

He froze, his lips pressed shut, his breathing halted. She leaned back, wondering if she'd misjudged.

"What are you doing?" he whispered.

"Distracting myself by using you."

His soft chuckle tickled across her mouth, even better, he didn't move away. "You don't give up do you?"

"I would have died if I had."

She regretted her words as soon as they left her lips. She expected the reminder of her past, the fact he saw her as a victim, to make him run away. It was what he did every time she got too close. Affected him.

This time though, he stayed. And he kissed her.

Her whole world exploded in to a whirl of sensation.

*

Viktor knew he should walk away. Run. Hide from this minx who called forth a tender side he never knew he was capable of. But how could he leave her? How could he deny her request to forget something that pained her? *She's a mission. A victim. Too young.* She was a woman looking for new memories. Looking for acceptance, whose life experiences gave her a wisdom and outlook on life that made her older than her years.

I can't say no. Didn't want to. He wanted to give her the comfort and distraction she searched for. Him and only him.

He kissed her. A light embrace. A touch of his lips to hers in soft exploration. His world tilted as the rightness of it slammed into him and left him reeling. Before he knew it, he lay atop her, her lush frame cradling his, his lips devouring hers with a hunger he couldn't control.

Reason tried to assert itself. He should slow down. She was new to this. An innocent…a seductress in disguise who wound her arms around his neck and nipped his lower lip when he tried to pull away.

A groan left him at her rough antics and she paused in her embrace. "I'm sorry, did I do something wrong?"

"No." *If only she knew how right she felt.*

"Oh good." She went back to sucking on his lower lip, and when he teased her with the tip of his tongue, she mewled in surprise before thrusting hers into his mouth, a sensual attack that had him grinding his lower body against her. Inexperienced, and even clumsy, despite her lack of skill, she aroused him in ways he'd never imagined. Roused every protective instinct he owned. And at the same time, all the tenderness he was capable of.

Bells went off as his hands stroked up and down her sides. A ringing tone he couldn't shake that went well with his addled mind.

Wait. Ringing. A phone.

He pulled away and she let out a sound of protest.

"What are you doing?" She regarded him with a pout.

He glanced away. "I need to answer that."

"I need you."

Three little words, and yet they almost undid him. But years of dedication to his work held sway – barely. He rolled off of her lush, welcoming body, every inch of him protesting. He made the mistake of looking back at her, her golden eyes at half-mast with passion, her lips swollen from the kiss.

He started to understand the attraction of dereliction of duty. For the first time ever he didn't want to do the right thing. He wanted to do a dirty thing.

The phone rang again.

With a curse, he exited the room and with angry strides, made his way to the kitchen where he'd left his cell phone charging.

"What?" he barked into the receiver.

"I'm sorry. Is this a bad time?"

"Who is this?"

"It's Doctor Manners, the physician assigned to one of the groups of recovered shifters from the raid on the lab. Am I speaking to Viktor?"

"You are."

"Nice to finally meet you. I've heard great things about your work."

"I'd be a lot happier to meet you if it wasn't three o'clock in the morning," Viktor growled. It would have also helped if the bloody doctor didn't interrupt him from his sensual exploration of the woman who haunted his every waking and sleeping moment.

"We've got a problem at the safe house."

Some of his ire died down at the serious tone. "Why are you calling me then? Shouldn't you have contacted the emergency switchboard for reinforcements?"

"Not that kind of problem. I spoke to Kloe and she told me I should call you. She mentioned one of the rescued victims is in your care."

"Yes." Anxiety gnawed him at the mention of Renee. "What's this have to do with her?"

"One of the subjects we were monitoring went into convulsions and died about an hour or so ago. We can't figure out why. He seemed stable. And then..." The doctor tapered off, but his meaning was clear.

So a shifter with health problems died. It didn't mean anything. Delayed shock, a weak heart, any number of reasons could have led to the poor man's death. "What do you want?"

A heavy sigh hummed through the line. "To warn you? Have you watch her more closely? I don't know. I just thought you should be informed in case you noticed something."

"Like?"

"As I said, we didn't get much warning. But then again, it was nighttime, so we weren't monitoring as closely given the patient slept. Keep an eye on the basics, temperature, skin color, dilation of the eyes, sudden changes in mood."

Icy cold and not because of his reptile blood, but out of fear for his fox, he snarled, "I'm not a freaking nurse."

"I understand that. I can look at her if you prefer. Why don't you bring her in for some tests?"

"You won't hurt her?"

"No!" Judging by his tone, the doctor seemed taken aback. "Just some basic blood work. A physical exam. Nothing intrusive. Until we find out what killed the patient, I won't even know what to look for, but the more information we have the better. I should have had her in before, but I've kind of had my hands full and FUC didn't want to bring in more doctors than necessary."

Of course not, because then the shifter world might know FUC hadn't entirely done its job in protecting them from the forces of darkness.

"I'll be there first thing in the morning with Renee for the tests."

"Thank you."

Viktor hung up and turned at a small sound.

"Tests?" Fear tightened Renee's face and his heart lurched in response.

"Nothing that will hurt. I promise." Or he'd punch the good doctor in the snout.

"You won't leave me with them?"

"Not even for a second." He'd even hold her hand if he had to. And shoot anyone who said anything smart about it. "Come on, let's get you to bed."

The tension in her shoulders eased a little. "Can we still go on our trip?"

"Later than I originally intended, but yes." He led her back, not to her room, but to his. And not to continue where they left off, not with that fearful look in her eyes and tremble in her limbs. He took her to his bed, and tucked her in before sliding in behind her. Only a gator with no heart would have sent her off to worry alone. Crocs had more class than that. But he didn't have enough will power to stop himself from drawing her into his arms, spooning her in to him, and laying his chin on the top of her head.

However, while her breathing ended up evening out into the smooth cadence of sleep, he couldn't help but worry, worry that perhaps a bomb ticked inside her, one he couldn't disarm that could take her from him at any moment. It seemed no matter how many times he reminded himself she deserved better, that he needed to stay away, he couldn't fight the allure of his fox. But it was a battle he gladly lost.

Chapter Eleven

Waking up in Viktor's arms was a treat, even if he immediately rolled away once she chirped good morning. Leaving just after breakfast with him tightlipped and silent, to meet some doctor for some tests, ruined some of her elation. The idea of letting someone poke her, and do things to her like the scientists from the old lab made her tummy churn. Determined not to show too much fear – because she knew it bothered Viktor – she instead let her mind replay the events of the night before.

The dream, more vivid than any of her previous ones, elated her. Even she didn't have the imagination to conjure up the kidnapping, the French, or the clues to her past, evidence she belonged to someone. *I have a family.* And she wasn't alone in believing it. As they got ready to leave, she heard Viktor on the phone with Jessie, sharing what little nuggets Renee revealed. When she asked him what the chances were they'd find her missing mother, he wouldn't promise her anything, but she knew he'd do his darnedest to find answers.

Almost as exciting as the thought of finding her family was what happened when she woke from her nightmare. Viktor kissed her! Oh, the beautiful heat of it. Just remembering made her body tingle. She'd come so close to discovering the pleasure everyone hinted about. A pleasure she'd know before the end of the day. No matter what Viktor thought, she was going to have sex with him, even if she had to tie him down, stomp on his phone and figure it out herself.

Maybe then he'd stop trying to keep her away. Not that he did a great job in the first place. He never pushed her away when she used him as a shield against the things that scared her. Didn't dump her out of his lap when she climbed in to her spot as the car that picked them up eased out into the bright sunlight. Heck, he tucked her under his arm without urging when they exited the vehicle at their destination.

Walking into the plain brown building, only three stories made ugly by the bars on its windows, trepidation turned her happy thoughts into somber ones. She'd thought herself done with tests. Done with places designed to keep shifters locked away.

As if sensing her unease, Viktor leaned in to whisper, "Don't be scared. If you so much as flinch during these tests, I'm going to make the doctor's face say hello to my fist."

A giggle escaped her. "And if I cry?" she asked peering up at him.

The slit in his eyes narrowed and his lips went taut. "Then he dies."

Heart lightening, she didn't doubt his claim for a minute.

A tall male dressed in slacks and a blue shirt approached them. With his golden mane of hair, bright blue eyes and wide smile, he appeared nice.

"Viktor, I presume. I'm Dr. Manners," he said, holding out his hand.

Just went to show, appearances could be deceiving. Renee smooshed herself closer to Viktor's side. His arm tightened around her shoulders.

"Doctor. I've brought Renee as requested. But keep in mind, hurt her and I'll hurt you. She's been through enough."

"I'll be gentle. Promise. If you'll come with me, Renee, this won't take too long."

If the doctor thought it strange Viktor followed, he didn't say a word. Nor did he say anything when her croc stationed himself at the foot of the examination bed, glaring. To his credit, other than the occasional shake of his head and twitch of his lips, the doctor ignored her protector. Dr. Manners also kept his word. He palpated her body over her clothing, ignoring the low rumbling growl that came from Viktor.

Bending and extending her limbs in a variety of exercises, the doctor explained what he was doing before he did it, and her initial nervousness eased. It came back lightning quick though when he rolled out a trolley with needles and vials for blood.

Viktor immediately comforted her, standing at her back and sliding his arms around her middle. He let his mouth almost touch the lobe of her ear when he said, "Almost done. Once he gets some blood, I'm going to show you my cabin. And if you're a really good fox, I'll show you my beast."

"Really?" She tilted her head to the side to see if he was serious. His lips tilted into a smile and he nodded his head. Excited by the idea of meeting his animal, she barely noticed the pinch of the needle and next thing she knew, the doctor stepped away and declared, "We're finished here."

"That's it?" she asked, surprised.

"As I told Viktor last night, I just needed a sample of your blood and DNA, as well as a record of your current physical status. Something I could use for comparison with the other victims, and in case we run into something in the future."

"So she's alright?" Viktor asked.

Dr. Manners shrugged. "As far as I can tell. But, should anything change, even something minor like her temperature, skin color or smell, bring her right back."

"I will. Call me if there are any more incidents."

"Incidents?" Renee whispered. "What happened?"

"One of your cellmates died last night."

"Who?" she asked.

"The guy with one arm."

"Oh no." Dismay laced her words. Was it an accident? Had his body finally given up the fight? Or was something more sinister at work? Did the mastermind look to eradicate its mistakes? *Am I next?*

She didn't mention her fears to Viktor. Couldn't. She didn't want him to think she looked for reasons to scare herself, however, she couldn't stop the worry from gnawing at her. And even as they drove to the cabin, Viktor in the driver's seat and her forced to sit in the passenger, her previous elation didn't return.

But, her determination to have Viktor make love to her became stronger than ever. *If the mastermind is out there, looking to capture or destroy us, then I need to step up and take what I want. I refuse to die or return to my prison without having a taste of rapture first.*

And her more selfish reason. *I want to make him mine.*

Chapter Twelve

What's this? Project X081 survived! Tucked around the corner, disbelief almost toppled the miniature force of evil. Mastermind had wondered what happened to the prize in the collection, thought Project had died actually, given she did not appear in the safe house with the other prisoners.

But she lived and seemed to have acquired a personal bodyguard in the form of one astute FUC agent. Eavesdropping, while risky, proved a gold mine of information. So, Project planned a getaway with her croc. How perfect, and the timing couldn't have worked out better. The passcode to the computer system was cracked the night before when the safe house was in an uproar over a death. It seemed the formula to success needed a little more fine tuning. Tonight, the mastermind would try again.

First though, with the aid of a sleeping agent slipped into a coffee, little fingers typed a command on the liberated computer. Moreau industries, while the finest of establishments, wasn't the last bastion by any means. More minions awaited orders. With a transfer of some cash here, the revelation of a cache of weapons there, along with directions to a certain cabin's location and a missive to capture, Mastermind once again took control. Plotted the demise of enemies.

And even better, used FUC's own computer and resources to do so.

Muah-ha, oops, the guard woke. Time to leave and spy some more while waiting for nightfall and the next round of experiments.

Chapter Thirteen

Renee quite enjoyed the drive out to Viktor's cottage, the greenery lining the road, much more pleasing to the eye than endless tall buildings, flashing signs, concrete, and noise. While the conversation began stilted, fear quelling her tongue, as Viktor, jaw tense, drove, eventually, as the miles passed, they relaxed. To her surprise, Viktor didn't avoid answering her numerous questions, even the personal ones.

"Do you have a family?"

"Yes."

"Tell me about them." She really had to coax him to give her even the tiniest crumb.

"My mother is Anastasia. My father is Brian. I have three brothers, older than me. And one bratty sister. Happy?"

"Very." So it went. She queried. He gave her the basics. She bugged for more. He gave her a long suffering sigh, then spilled. It was great.

"So you actually celebrate birthdays?" she asked, when he mentioned his most embarrassing moment was when he accidentally knocked over the cake his mother baked for his brother onto his grandmother, who, slightly senile, flipped into her crocodile self and went after him to teach him a lesson on being careful.

"Not so much anymore. But when I was a kid, my mother made a big deal about them."

"I don't remember having a birthday. Actually, I don't recall ever having cake."

The car swerved. "What? But you've had dessert, right?"

"We got the occasional sweets over the years, usually snuck in by one of the guards or nurses who felt sorry for us. I had vanilla pudding once. It was yummy."

"I wished you'd told me that before," he grumbled. "I don't keep that kind of stuff at my place because it's not healthy. But I would have bought some for you, if I'd known."

Renee smiled. "I don't mind. Food is food. Actually," she revised. "It's not. Your food is marvelous compared to the goo they fed us. I can't imagine anything tasting better than that."

The subject changed after that, but it remained comfortable, even if she shocked him a few more times with her lack of experience in certain matters, and too much experience in others.

He made one stop in a small town, mostly because she just had to go! Emerging from the washroom, that was a far cry from the pristine one at Viktor's house, she caught him slamming the trunk of the car shut.

"Did you buy something?"

"Just a few extra supplies. Nothing for you to worry about. Let's go. We're almost there."

The car left civilization behind and wound up a road bordered by the tallest trees imaginable. The asphalt turned to gravel, and the vehicle bounced to her giggling delight. When they emerged at last from the canopy of foliage, she clapped her hands in delight at the sight of the cabin. With a frame comprised of logs, a shingle roof and a wide porch, it appeared inviting.

"Oh, it's so pretty."

"Functional," he corrected.

"Pretty," she stubbornly reiterated. A tree in the front yard with a tire hanging from a rope caught her attention. "What's that for?"

"Swinging."

When she threw him a puzzled look, he smiled with all his pointed teeth. "Come on, little fox. Time for you to be a kid."

He slinked out of the car, and Renee followed, only to falter at the open sky overhead. Big, and blue, it made her heart race. *I really need to get over this fear.* No one else hesitated at the sight of all that vast space. She'd not noticed anything falling from it to hit people on the head. She needed to fight this terror.

Viktor stood a few feet away, patiently waiting, hand outstretched.

Biting her lip, and ignoring the looming sky, that could suck her into space should gravity decide to fail, she trotted over to him.

He didn't mention her bravery, but the smile on his lips spoke for him. Clasping her hand, he led her to the tire contraption, and with hand gestures and words, explained how it worked. Seated on the sun warmed black rubber, hands holding onto the rope, she let out a squeal when he pushed her. She soared up. Then down. He shoved her again and she laughed.

"Look at me. I'm flying!"

*

Look at her indeed. Cheeks flushed, eyes brimming with delight and her open mouth spilling laughter, Viktor stared, completely and utterly entranced. A bomb could have exploded and he might still have stood there, slack jawed and drooling at the enticing sight.

Damn.

Why did that keep happening?

Leaving her to spin like a mad top, he kept an eye on her as he carted the boxes of food and luggage into the cabin. He doubted danger would court them so quickly after their arrival, and given the way he ensure nothing followed them, but he left nothing to chance.

On his last trip for supplies, he exited the house only to see the swing empty, and not a fox in sight.

An unfamiliar sensation, one almost of panic, suffused him. "Renee!"

A warm body tackled him from the side and instinct kicked in. Before he knew it, he'd pinned the attacker to the ground, but he reined in his strength as he realized who played games with him.

"What have I told you about surprising me?" he growled.

"If you don't want me to do it, then stop making it so fun," she replied with a smirk. She squirmed under him, not to get away, he noted. His cock approved of her methods.

"Bad fox."

"Shouldn't you be impressed I got the drop on you?"

He couldn't help but smile at that. "Fine. I'll give you that. You sneak really well. While we're up here, maybe I'll give you some defense moves to go with that skill."

"Yay!"

"But not right yet," he said, unable to stop himself from kissing the tip of her nose. "First, we need to get settled in and get some food in our bellies. You'll need your strength for tonight."

"Ooh, I like the sound of that," she exclaimed.

"Remember that later." Later when he got her to strip and tried to get her to change into her animal. And no, it wasn't an excuse to get her naked. He really wanted to see if her alter ego truly was stuck.

As Renee explored the cabin, Viktor prepared them a simple dinner on the barbecue; steaks with a mesquite seasoning, corn on the cob dripping with butter, and a crusty French bread he'd grabbed in town, along with his other surprise.

Renee dug in with gusto, a trait he admired. Too many women obsessed about their weight and made themselves miserable eating like birds. Renee though… She treated each meal like a trip to ecstasy, groaning her delight, eating every last bit, rubbing her belly and sighing with content.

If food gave her that reaction, just how intense was she during sex? The temptation to find out was an agony worse than the knife wound he'd received in the back from a botched military maneuver.

Dinner finished, dishes washed, and night falling, he finally brought out his surprise. Renee eyed the white box.

"What is it?"

"Open it and see."

Flipping up the lid, she gasped. Then cried. Shit.

"It's a cake. For me," she whispered as tears rolled down her cheeks.

Nestled in the box, was a chocolate cake iced in mocha, decorated with pink frosting flowers and with the words, 'Happy Birthday, Renee!'

Viktor pulled out the candles he'd also bought and placed them on top before lighting them. He then – thanking the swamp gods that no one watched – sang the birthday song while she cried.

The song ended, and as the flames still danced, he murmured, "Make a wish." She blew the candles out with a lusty breath and he couldn't help hoping her wish involved him.

"Thank you," she whispered turning bright eyes to him.

"You're welcome. But the cake isn't the only surprise." He pulled out a gift bag and handed it to her.

At her questioning look, he just smiled. Waited. Then snickered as she held up the present.

The t-shirt depicted a crocodile, fanged and cartoonish with a big smile on his face and a rounded belly. The caption underneath read, 'I came to see the crocodiles. I stayed for dinner.'

Renee snickered, then laughed. Eyes crinkling, Viktor joined her.

"I can't believe you bought this."

Me either. He'd wanted to get her a gift, but the small store mostly had grocery items, except for a display of tourist t-shirts that bore funny expressions and images. That he'd even bought one said more than he cared to admit.

"Well, it's not a birthday without a present. But put the shirt aside for the moment, time for your first piece of chocolate cake."

He sliced them each a piece and dished them onto small plates, but forgot to eat his when Renee closed her eyes and moaned in absolute ecstasy at her first bite.

"Good?"

Mouth full of another piece, she nodded her head.

"Better than my cooking?"

"Taste for yourself." The devilish glint in her eye should have warned him, but where she was concerned, none of his senses worked right. She leaned in and pressed her mouth to his before he could blink. Mouth parted slightly, he couldn't help but taste the rich mocha on her lips. It roused his hunger. Fingers laced at the back of her head, her drew her closer to him, meshing his mouth to hers firmly, letting her sweet flavored tongue slide along his.

Best cake ever.

They continued to kiss even after the morsel disappeared, and it was with reluctance, he drew away. He grinned in male satisfaction when it took her a moment to open her eyes and come to her senses.

"That was *yummy*," she said in a husky murmur that almost had him shoving another piece in her mouth.

"I'm glad you liked it. And it'll taste even better later after we come back from the woods."

A frown creased her brow. "Why are we going into the woods?"

To get you naked. For a purpose that didn't involve sex, yet. "It's time you met your fox."

Chapter Fourteen

"Why are we out here again?" Renee grumbled slapping at yet another mosquito daring to hover too close. She'd have much preferred to stay in the kitchen, eating the decadent cake, devouring Viktor's even more delectable lips, and then moving on to a physical activity involving less clothes. And not the shapeshifting kind like he seemed intent on forcing.

"We are out here because I think your ability to shapeshift – "

"You mean lack of."

"– is related to your memory loss."

"So what?" She also couldn't remember her name when he kissed her, but that didn't bother her either. How had they gone from delicious dessert and kissing, to outside by some wet and smelly marsh? "Did it ever occur to you that I just can't do it?"

"Of course you can. You're a shifter for swamp's sake. Shifters shift."

"I disagree. And I would also like to note that while this bog might be familiar turf for crocodiles, aren't foxes more at home in the forest?" Actually, according to her body, she'd find herself most at home in his bed, naked, with him on top. Despite her lack of experience, she caught on quick, and found herself intrigued after having watched, with wide eyes, the romantic liaisons depicted in movies and TV shows over the last few days.

"Ah, but if by chance this does work and you do shift, if you bolt because you get scared, I'll have more luck following you in the marsh than I would on land."

She wrinkled her nose. "But it's gooey looking."

"But good for the skin. You should thank me. Women pay good money for mud baths."

"They do not," she exclaimed.

"Do too."

Her skeptical look didn't make him back down. She shook her head. "That's just nuts."

"Stop stalling. I want you to concentrate on calling your fox."

"It won't work. I've tried and tried to shift. I just can't do it."

"What if I gave you the right incentive?" His serious look didn't give a hint as to what kind of incentive he meant.

"Like what?"

"I'll make you dinner."

"You do that already."

"No, I'll make *you* dinner."

"You just said that."

He sighed. "I meant, I'll finish what got interrupted the other night. What we started again over the cake."

Oh. *Oooh.* Now she understood. And she wanted the prize. However, his capitulation seemed too easy. "I thought you said I was too young."

"You are."

"And what about the fact protecting me is your mission?"

"Do you want to do this or not?" he snapped.

"Testy, testy. Is that the old ornery croc thing coming out that Miranda warned me about?"

"I'll show you old," he growled. He advanced on her with a look in his eye that probably sent his prey skittering. It shot a shiver down her spine. She stood her ground.

"Should I get naked for this?" she asked.

A quirk tilted his lips. "If you want. Myself, I prefer to strip before shifting. Nothing worse than a crocodile wearing Fruit of the Loom briefs."

She giggled, a laughter that cut short when he yanked his shirt over his head and revealed the chest she'd come to think of as hers. He placed the fabric over a branch before kicking off his boots. He pulled a revolver from the back of his pants and laid it carefully on the ground.

"No holster?" she asked.

"Holster's are for pussies and bears. Crocs aren't afraid of a little danger."

"Then why does the knife have a sheath?" she inquired pointing to the velcroed band around his upper bicep.

"Because I prefer to shave on my terms," he replied with a grin. "Are you asking all these questions to try and distract me?"

"Who me?" She widened her eyes.

He chuckled, but she couldn't utter a sound when knife put aside, he placed his hands on the clasp to his jeans. Knowing she'd get to see him in all his naked glory in a moment just about made her swoon. She definitely wet the crotch of her panties, and her heart went into serious overdrive.

Eyes locked on his slow strip tease, she didn't even blink as he undid the buttons, revealing bulging dark fabric.

"Must you stare?" he growled.

"I'd videotape it if I could."

He groaned. "You'll be the death of me."

"I hope not. You made me a promise."

"A promise that I'll have a hard time keeping if you keep staring at me like that. A croc's only got so much patience."

"Then stop taking so long."

A heartbeat later, he'd shed his pants, shucked his briefs and stood there in all his splendid, very naked and erect glory.

Knees weak, she leaned against the tree behind her. "You're beautiful," she sighed.

"Can't we go with something a little more manly like handsome or fearsome?"

"But you are beautiful." And he was each delineated muscle a thing to admire. The perfect blend of wide shoulders, broad chest leading to tapered hips and muscled thighs. Even his prick, bobbing, thick and, yes fearsome looking, was beautiful. The heat coursing in her veins rose a few notches.

"Your turn," he replied in a voice grown thick. She held his gaze, heart stuttering as his slitted eyes lit with passion.

Slowly, with the same decadence he showed her, she stripped, each burning glance of his eyes igniting her skin, tightening her awareness until she almost panted. And they'd not even touched.

When she stood naked before him, he swallowed hard. She waited for him to say something. Or better, do something. Touch her. Kiss her. Make love to her. Anything.

When he finally whispered, she strained to hear. "Perfection." She flushed at his compliment.

Still, though, he didn't move. Didn't give her what his body and eyes promised. It seemed she'd have to wrestle him into submission.

Hips swaying, in a hopefully seductive manner she'd studied on television, she approached him.

He shook his finger at her. "Not yet, my naughty fox. First you need to change shape."

"I'd rather wear your shape."

A tremor went through him. "I'm trying to help you here."

"Help me then. Help me put out this ache I've got between my legs." Having not been taught the niceties of society, she said exactly what came to mind.

He groaned. "Not yet. Not until you try. I'll go first. This is what we call a half shift." Before her eyes, she watched him molt, his human skin darkening, and she'd guess hardening, as scales emerged to cover his tanned skin. He held up his hands as his fingers turned a greenish-grey and sprouted claws. His thighs thickened, and, holy moly, a tail came into existence, whipping behind him.

As for his face, the jaw and nose elongated into a snout, his hair virtually disappeared, but the same yellow eyes she'd come to know regarded her. His voice, when it emerged, had a guttural roughness she didn't find unpleasant.

"In my half form, I keep my basic humanoid shape and can move on two legs. My skin is harder. My reflexes faster. And my strength increased." He flexed an arm and an impressive bulge popped up. "Your turn."

She sighed. "It won't work. But if you insist." Closing her eyes, she fisted her hands at her side and wished with all her might to change shapes. It wasn't that she couldn't sense that other half of herself inside, she could, it just didn't want to come out and play.

"Are you concentrating on your fox?"

Truthfully? "No. I'm thinking I'd much rather be eating some more cake."

"Try harder."

"Why? Who cares if I can shapeshift? Why is everyone so obsessed with my lack of ability?"

Viktor morphed back into his human form. "Who else pressured you?"

"The scientists and doctors. They said I was being stubborn. Doing it on purpose to screw with their tests."

"And?"

"And what? I wasn't. I just can't shift. Not that they believed me. They tried everything. Electroshock, which tickles after you've gone through it for a while. Drugs, some which made me so hungry. One doctor hit me a few times when I couldn't do it, but he did it too hard I guess because I passed out and woke up in my cell. They must have fired him because I never saw him again."

Before she could take in a breath, Viktor held her in his arms, his skin cool against hers. He gazed down at her, fierce and angry. "I'll kill them all," he growled, his eyes glowing with inner fire.

"Why?"

"Because they hurt you. I'll shoot them in the kneecaps and make them crawl. Hook them to some booster cables and clip them to a power line. Inject poison into their veins."

"And then?"

"I'll kill them."

She sighed. "That is so romantic."

He snorted. "It was meant to be a vicious promise of vengeance."

"I know. But it's still almost poetic."

"You're nuts," he said with a shake of his head. "But I like it," he admitted with a rueful smile.

"So you like me?" She held her breath as soon as the words slipped past her lips. Would he answer?

He took a while to reply and her heart sank with each second that passed.

"I do," he finally said in a tone so low she almost missed it. "I shouldn't, but swamp help me, I do."

Her heart went from a stuttering stop to full speed. "Really? You're not saying that just because you feel sorry for me."

"I wouldn't lie about something like that. Especially not to you."

"So, what does this mean?"

"It doesn't change the fact you're still too young for me and that my job is to protect you."

"I hear that boys mature more slowly than girls, or so Miranda claims. If that's the case, then really, we're not that far apart. Actually," she pressed herself tighter to him. "We're pretty darned close. And I can't think of a better way to protect me than if you're with me."

"You don't mean that. You've barely seen anything of the world. There's much better prospects out there than an old croc who can't learn new tricks."

"But none of them have the experience needed to protect me. The skills to take care of my body."

He groaned. "You just won't give up."

"So give in. Please, Viktor. Teach me. Touch me. Show me what if feels like to have a man inside of me." And not just any man, but Viktor, the only man to ever rouse her erotic interest and make her speak so wantonly.

"And if I don't?"

She ran a finger down his chest, the smoothness of his chest fascinating. "Would you truly condemn me like that?"

"I'm not the right man for you."

"You're the only man for me," she whispered. "Don't you understand? Nobody else has ever made me feel like my whole body is on fire. Nobody else makes me feel safe and beautiful. Only you make have the power to make me beg. Don't let me go back to my prison without having tasted what only you can give me."

"You're not going back. Never. I swear it," he growled. "I will kill anyone who tries."

"And what if it's death that comes to take me instead? What if it's my own body that betrays me?"

"I won't let it."

A sad smile pulled at her lips. "You can't stop it. No one can ever truly erase what was done to me and the others, or reverse the effects. I might live a hundred years, or die before this night is done. Nothing you do or promise can change that. But you can give me this. Show me what it's like to be a woman in all ways." She raised eyes shining with tears to meet his. "Show me a pleasure on par with chocolate cake, and shopping and all the other wondrous things you've introduced me to."

A crooked, yet tender smile curved his lips. "I'm better than any cake."

"Prove it." When he hesitated still, she kissed him, putting all of her passion, her need, her affection for him in the embrace. Would he reject her? Would he…

To her delight, with a groan of surrender, he melted. He took over the kiss, his mouth slanting across her lips and taking control. With firm nibbles and caresses, he took the fire in her body and turned it into an inferno.

Awash in sensations, from his tongue sliding along hers, to his hands roaming the length of her body, she didn't notice when he lay them down on a bough of soft grass that bent under their weight. She welcomed the heavy, hardness of his body as he covered hers, her thighs parting naturally so he could settle between them.

He kissed her like a man starving, meeting her passion and leaving her hungry for more. Not knowing what to do with her hands, she gripped his shoulders, the feel of his muscles tense under her touch, his skin warming to meet the temperature of hers, a delight to her senses. As for the weapon between his legs…it pulsed, hot and hard against her pelvis, trapped between their bodies, a curiosity she longed to explore.

A soft moan of dismay left her when he tore his mouth from hers. She was about to protest when his lips touched the soft skin of her neck, then travelled lower, branding her flesh. She gasped, and a jolt of pure pleasure shot to her sex when he brushed across a nipple. Cried out when he took the taut peak into his mouth and sucked. But enjoyable as that was, it couldn't compare to the shocking intensity of sensation when he grazed his pointed teeth over her tight nub.

She couldn't help bucking against him, the hungry passion controlling her limbs. He grunted, and for a moment she thought she'd done something wrong, until he murmured, "You taste even sweeter than I imagined."

He fantasized about me?

The elation at this words lasted only briefly as once again, the fury of their lovemaking overtook her senses and thoughts. While he played with her nipples, nipping and sucking them in turn, he shifted his body to allow his hand to tickle down her stomach, trace through the fur on her mound, and then to lightly trace her sex.

Again, without volition, her body bucked, her hips arching, begging for more of his touch. He stroked her, his finger slipping between the folds of her pussy, touching the dampness within, before withdrawing.

Breath held in expectation, of what, she didn't know, she let out a mewl of protest. His lips caught her cry as his finger returned, sliding back and forth against her core before finding the nub just above it. He pressed against it, and she cried out. He swallowed the sound and rubbed again, swift firm strokes, back and forth over the spot. Faster and faster, the pleasure inside her twisted and spun. Her entire body thrummed with excitement, and within her, the bliss went taut and she panted for breath, wondering, waiting. What was happening? What...

The orgasm, a sweeping wave of ecstasy that roared through her body, left her soundless, her mouth open wide in a silent scream. She couldn't hear, see, just feel, feel the waves of pleasure wracking her body, his murmurs of encouragement, the soft caress of his hands and lips.

Never once, in all her musings, did she imagine anything as wondrous as what occurred. So mind blowing. Shattering. And Viktor wasn't done.

Before she could register what he did, he slid down her body until his mouth blew softly on her trembling sex. The words, 'What are you doing?" clung to her tongue, but never left them. Instead, she screamed as he licked her in her most intimate of spots. Licked her until she thought she would die of pleasure.

*

Once Viktor started making love to Renee, unable to resist her plea, unable to resist her, he couldn't stop. Her kisses drugged him. Her body entranced him. And her orgasm at his hands? Just about made him come like a boy with no control instead of a man with ice running in his veins.

Everything about her was perfect. Especially the taste. Nestled between her thighs, he devoured her nectar, flicking the tip of his tongue against her clit, the most he could manage because of his crocodile nature. Damned short tongue. It still drove her wild, which in turn frenzied him. He could have licked her all day, made her come until she was hoarse if it weren't for the throb of his cock.

But was she ready to take that part of him?

Not stopping his oral torture of her nub, he slid a finger into her, and gasped. Tight. So nice, wet and tight. He slid another digit in, stretching her and pushing to get deeper, then pausing at the barrier in his path, the sign of her innocence.

A virgin. Shit.

For a moment, clarity returned. What was he doing? Seducing an innocent? She should give that prize to someone more deserving. Not an old jaded croc like him.

As if sensing his hesitation, she spoke. "Please, Viktor. Don't stop now. Please."

Honor and the right thing couldn't win against her plea – or his selfish desire. He wanted to be the first, and only one to take the gift she offered.

Her ardor slightly dampened as he went through his epiphany, he worked at bringing her back to a fever pitch. He thrust his fingers into her, loosening her, hopefully enough, to take him without too much discomfort. He licked her until she tugged at his scalp and her juices made everything slippery. Then, when she sat on the brink of climax again, he positioned himself over her, the head of his cock nudging the entrance to her sex.

"Are you –"

He didn't get to finish asking because her legs wrapped around his shanks, her body arched up, and she drew him inside. Surprised, he didn't do a thing to stop it, and when he hit the barrier in his path…he tore through, hoping the swiftness would not prolong the pain.

But if she noticed it, she gave no sign. She panted without pause, her fingers dug into his shoulders and her hips rocked, urging him on. Despite her inexperience, her body knew what it wanted. Primal need drove her, and she met his thrusts, her sex tight and welcoming around him.

Lost in the glory of her body, Viktor pumped, a slow cadence in and out. However, with the way she clenched around him, her inner sex quivering, her cries mounting again in intensity, he soon pounded at her flesh, unable to halt his frenzy.

And she yelled for more, her nails raking his back, her hooded eyes glowing with passion, and her teeth, hot damn, sharp fangs that pinched when she yanked him down and bit.

Pain, pleasure, and the climax racing through her pulled him in for one final thrust before he spilled his seed.

Sweet gods of the swamp. For a moment he thought he'd die at the intense pleasure wracking his body.

Before he could thank Renee, kiss her, and contemplate round two, something pricked him in the ass. Back. Arm.

Ambushed. Shit. He couldn't even manage a roar before he collapsed on top of her.

Chapter Fifteen

Renee scented the intruders a moment before Viktor collapsed on her, heavy and unresponsive. Passion still clinging to her, her senses muddled, she didn't immediately react.

But when Viktor's limp frame was yanked off hers, she sprang up with a scream.

Prick. Jab. Prick.

She peeked down at the tufted darts peppering her body. "Ow?" she said.

"Why isn't she going down?" someone asked. It occurred to her she should answer as she caught the sound of tranquilizer guns getting refilled.

"Um, you can't sedate me," she offered as she peered around.

The situation didn't look good. About a half dozen men surrounded her and an unconscious Viktor, who also wore several of the sleeping darts. Relief he lived made some of her tension ease. But it came right back when a scruffy man, who smelled an awful lot like a dog, said, "Get the rope. We'll truss her up then since she won't go to sleep like a good girl."

"Stay away from me," she said, holding her hands up.

"Or else what?"

"Or–or–" Renee chewed her lower lip as nothing came to mind. Viktor was down for the count. She didn't wear a stitch of clothing. Possessed no weapon – although even if she did, it wouldn't have done her any good. Exactly what were her options?

If she ran, what would happen to Viktor? She couldn't leave him alone. Sighing, she did what years of prison taught her. She gave in to the inevitable and held out her hands.

It seemed freedom wasn't hers to keep after all. *Well, this sucks.*

If only Viktor had taken the time to teach her how to fight. She could have vanquished the smelly kidnappers, saved her crocodile and woken him with kisses.

Instead, she stumbled along with her hands tied in front of her, mouth gagged with a piece of thick tape, poked by rifles, accompanied by the hunters who joked about their fine catch. More worrisome, they discussed what a good time they'd have in town after they sold her and Viktor to a store specializing in women's fashion accessories. It seemed fox fur and crocodile leather were in high demand.

But the joke was on them. While they could scent her vixen nature, they didn't know she couldn't shift which meant their big money dream of turning her into a fur stole would never happen. Yay for her small victory. Boo for the fact they intended to turn Viktor into a pair of boots. Maybe even a purse.

Somehow she didn't think he'd like that at all.

As soon as she saw the cages, she upgraded their big trouble status to really screwed, but the true terror didn't hit until she heard the word *mastermind*. It seemed these hunters of shifters weren't random. They worked for the very person she'd hoped to escape.

I don't want to go back to my prison.

Hold on a second. Why did she automatically assume the bad guys would win? Sure, Viktor was currently naked, unconscious and getting locked in a cage. It didn't mean he couldn't still save them both.

She had faith in him. He'd promised to always protect her. If anyone could get them out of this mess, Viktor could.

And she believed that up until the moment they shot him.

*

The bore of a rifle – the shape, something Viktor knew well – poked him in the back and he jolted awake. Without pausing to think, Viktor sprang to his feet, a cloud in his mind dulling his senses, to discover himself…in a cage.

What the hell? How had he arrived here?

His second thought was, Renee! The last thing he recalled was reaching nirvana buried in her body, then, the stings as someone ambushed them while he was occupied.

I should be shot for being so stupid. He'd let his dick overrule his common sense and got caught. But who cared about him, where was Renee?

Before he could look for her, the jerk off with the gun poked the barrel of his weapon at Viktor's naked belly.

"Well, well. The gator finally wakes.

"It's croc, you ill-bred excuse for a – " Viktor eyed his captor; about five foot nine, greasy brown hair, and a distinct smell of coon. "Ring eyed bandit."

"What do you know, the lizard can smell."

"Even a vulture would smell your piss poor excuse for an animal."

The gun poked deeper and the finger on the trigger tightened. "Mouthy bastard aren't you."

"Where's Renee?"

A grin split the miscreant's lips, a gap-toothed smile with way too much malice. "Your girlfriend is over

122

there. The drugs didn't work on her so we had to use other methods to keep her quiet."

Whirling, Viktor saw Renee hogtied hand and foot in another cage a few yards away. A gag covered her mouth and her eyes were wide with fright.

"Let. Her. Go." The rage pumped through him at her demise. How could he have screwed up so bad? He'd let pleasure override his common sense. Let his guard down because of his intrigue for a fox, and look where it got them? Drugged and caught like the newest of recruits. He needed to fix this. Now.

"Oh, she's not going anywhere, lizard man. I've got someone who's promised me good money for that there piece of ass. Too much money for me to give a shit what you want. Heck, they offered me even more money when I mentioned what price I could get for a fox's fur."

"Who? Who's paying you?" Viktor's blood ran colder than usual. Only one person would have an interest in Renee. Mastermind.

"Shouldn't you be more worried about yourself, crocodile? The boss don't want nothing to do with you. But it seems a shame to waste your leather. I've got a buddy who deals in skins. Reptile skins. Those rich broads in the fancy houses love those genuine purses and boots."

Viktor stalled as he tried to analyze the situation and come up with a way to free them both. "That plan would work a lot better if you hadn't caught me in my human shape."

"You'll shift if you know what's good for you."

"Not likely."

"Oh you will cause if you don't, you get to watch as I put it to your girlfriend. Is she a screamer? Maybe I'll take the gag off and find out."

Icy fear transitioned into a cold rage. "Don't you lay a finger on her."

"Or else what? In case you ain't noticed, I've got you in a fucking cage, lizard. There ain't a goddamned thing you can do about it either."

Eyeing the bars and the lock keeping the door shut, Viktor laughed, a low, mirthless sound. "Is this the best you've got? I'd start running now if I were you, because once I get out, you can forget about mercy. I'm hungry for some fresh meat."

The swaggering confidence waned as the coon stepped back from the cage. Only belatedly did the hunter recall his gun. He raised it, aiming it high on Viktor's chest. "Even if you could get out, you ain't bullet proof."

"But I heal real fast so you better hope your aim is good." With a flex of his muscles, Viktor shifted into his half shape, his leathery skin affording some protection if the coon did fire, but even better, it gave him the strength and weight needed to slam against the bars and snap the lock. Stumbling out, his captor's eyes widened in shock, but he didn't panic as much as Viktor would have liked. The prick fired at him!

Viktor didn't flinch when the first bullet grazed his arm. The kidnapper – who wanted to turn him into some fucking purse – went down under him. The coon tried to shift out of his human shape, probably hoping his smaller size would allow him to escape. A hard chomp on his neck and the coon stopped struggling.

Too quick of a death for the scumbag, but given the camp showed signs of more than one hunter, and Renee was probably frightened out of her mind, he chose speed over the pleasure of making the dirtbag scream.

Springing to his feet, he took a quick glance around before he strode over to the cage which held Renee and wrenched the door open. Shifting back to his human shape, he then tugged her into his arms, holding her trembling body.

"I'm so sorry, Renee. I should have never taken you out here with no protection."

She shook her head and mumbled something."

"This is going to sting," he warned before pulling the tape from her mouth.

But it wasn't pain making her scream when her lips were free, but, "Watch out behind you!"

Too late. Still muddled from the tranquilizers, he never heard the coon's friends approaching, but he felt it when they shot him, the sting of buckshot spraying across his back.

"Run," he gasped, shoving her to her feet. But still bound, she could only lie there.

Another shot sent him reeling face first onto the hard ground. His chest ached when he breathed and his vision dimmed. But he still managed to whisper, through bubbles of blood "I'm sorry. I failed you."

*

Shock kept Renee silent as Viktor collapsed on the ground, bleeding and unconscious – *please don't be dead.* Things went so horribly wrong so quick. One moment, she silently cheered as she watched Viktor kill the hunter who'd stayed behind to guard her. The next, her lover lay bleeding on the ground.

From the woods, the hunter's friends emerged, dressed in camouflaged fatigues, weapons aimed at her and her poor, dying croc.

"Make a move and we'll shoot."

As if she needed the warning. She well knew the rules when dealing with mercenaries. *Do as you're told and maybe you won't get hurt.* It was why she didn't fight when they initially bound her wrists and ankles, didn't struggle when they taped her mouth to silence her sobs.

But she could have handled returning to her prison of a life if they'd left Viktor alone. She would have promised anything to keep him safe. Instead, though, he bled on the ground and death approached carrying a shotgun and a sneer. *And I don't know what to do.*

"Fuck the few hundred bucks we'll get from his skin. He's too much trouble. We've got the girl. Kill him."

Weapons raised and aimed at her helpless lover. Renee saw no mercy in their eyes, only death.

Fear coalesced into anger. *How dare they!* The anger burned and churned inside her. A red haze dropped over her eyes.

"Don't. Touch. Him," she growled in a voice she didn't recognize.

"You mean like this?" A weapon fired and a red splotch bloomed on Viktor's thighs, already unconscious, he didn't even flinch. But the casual shot sent her over the edge.

A scream of rage burst from her and she jumped to her feet, snapping the bonds holding her without effort.

Every inch of her vibrated and still her fury grew with each inhalation as the coppery scent of Viktor's blood assailed her.

"Shoot!" screamed their leader, spittle flying. "Shoot her before she –"

The leader of the hunters didn't finish his sentence. In one fell swoop, she silenced him. Crunching her jaws, eating her snack, she eyed the other puny creatures holding black sticks. One of them made a loud noise and a moment later something stung her.

She roared. They ran. Her ears perked up. *Prey!* Tail high, she chased, their scents easy to follow. She caught a fleeing figure with a gleeful pounce. She ate, savoring the fresh meal. Yum.

Chapter Sixteen

It took Mason, accompanied by Dr. Manners and several of the best agents FUC had to offer, a few hours to make it to Viktor's cabin. When his croc buddy failed to check in, they'd immediately gotten on their way because Viktor wouldn't miss calling without good reason. Mason just couldn't believe someone would have gotten the drop on his friend and mentor. Even when confronted with the empty cabin – everything in its place, no sign of a struggle – Mason couldn't allow himself to believe that he man who trained him was perhaps in trouble.

Viktor always came out ahead. The man possessed uncanny instincts and was deadly with a gun, and even more so with a knife.

But then again, his single buddy was perhaps distracted by a certain redhead. Mason had never seen Viktor behave so out of character. Letting a woman stake a claim on his lap? The Viktor he knew was more likely to shove her off. Or had, until Renee. As for taking her to his cabin on the pretext of getting her to relax so she could shapeshift? Mason never heard a bigger load of crock in his life. Viktor never took women to his private haven. But he took the fox.

On the hunt for the croc and his charge, was Mason going to accidentally interrupt something naked and sweaty? He hoped not. He'd just eaten some delicious honey buns and he'd hate to bring them back up.

"Cabin is clear," he announced to the men milling around the structure. "Let's fan out and see if we can pick up a trail. Maybe he met a croc bigger than him and got hurt." Or the love bug bit him.

Dr. Manners went to follow him into the forest when Mason halted him. "Where are you going, doc?"

"With you, of course."

"You any good at tracking?"

"No, but if there're injuries, my presence could make a difference."

"Viktor's a shifter and a tough son of a bitch. Short of a blast to the head or decapitation, he'll survive."

"Have you ever seen a broken leg heal crooked when it's not set correctly?" Dr. Manners asked. "It's not pretty for anyone. Having me along could make a difference. Not to mention, we have no idea how Renee's ability to heal might have gotten affected by her testing."

"Valid points, but we don't know what we might run into."

To his credit, the doctor didn't back down. "I might not have the same training as you, but I can take care of myself."

"What if we run into some of the mastermind's henchmen?" Mason asked.

A smile curved the doctor's lips. "Then it's a good thing my beast likes fresh meat. Shall we?"

With a snort of mirth, Mason let his nose lead the way. Lucky for him, his keen sense of smell picked up a trail. It led down to the marsh, then to a crumpled pile of long grass where he got the distinct scent of his old unit buddy getting lucky. But it was the feathered dart on the ground that raised his hackles.

Dropping to his knees, he lifted the missile and sniffed, the distinct medical aroma a bad sign. Someone drugged them. But who? Regular human hunters who thought they'd caught themselves a large prize? Or deadly shifters, ones with nefarious reasons?

Pulling his cell phone from his belt, Mason sent out a text to the other units. *Hostiles in area. Proceed with caution.* He also texted them the exact coordinates of his location.

"You still with me, doc?"

Loosening his tie, the doctor unbuttoned the top of his shirt. "I don't give up easily, bear. Lead the way."

As Mason jogged along the trail that no one bothered to hide, he called his wife via his Bluetooth.

"What's up?" she said immediately answering, the sound of her typing in the background the sign of her multitasking ability. By all the honey in the world, he loved how she used that skill in the bedroom.

"Up? Not me, that's for sure. Viktor and his charge seem to have been abducted."

"By who?"

"I'm not sure yet. But they came prepared with darts laced with some kind of drug. Sedative I'd wager. No blood though, which is a good sign. It means they wanted them undamaged."

"Do you think it was the mastermind? How though? I'm sure Viktor didn't tell anyone he and Renee were heading there. It was spur of the moment."

"Well, I knew as did you," Jessie answered. "And Kloe. But that's it as far as I know."

"I knew they were going to his cabin," Manners offered, apparently able to hear Jessie's side of the conversation. Privacy didn't exist for shifters in close proximity. "They talked about it when they came to the safe house for some tests."

"We have a mole," Mason growled.

"Not for long," Jessie announced. "I'll check the safe house phones and computers for breaches to the outside."

"Sounds good. I'll call you back when we find them."

"Oh, no you won't. You keep that line open so I can hear what's going on."

"Bossy swan." He said it affectionately.

"Love you too," she sassed.

Mason slowed his pace as a metallic tang filled his senses. Not far ahead, there was blood. "Stay behind me, doc." Inching forward, Mason trained his ears, listening for any sound of a possible ambush. He kept breathing deep, looking for a scent that didn't belong. However, the aroma of death permeated everything.

Signs of violence began to litter the path. Lonely shoe over here. Tattered remnants of a shirt. Blood. Cracked tree limbs. More blood. It looked like a violent tornado went tearing through the forest taking out – *sniff, sniff* – shifters along its way. Or did he gaze upon the remains of a rampaging croc?

Nah. He didn't for a moment think Viktor did it because his friend tended to make clean kills, saving the maiming only for special occasions.

Inhaling again, Mason tried to sift the scents. The distinct tang unique to shifters rose above the coppery one of blood, however, he couldn't pinpoint which of the many smells caused the destruction.

"What did this?" the doctor asked, kneeling to grasp a long russet strand caught on the bore of a tree.

Given the length of the hair, Mason didn't entirely want to know.

"Did what?" Jessie asked.

He didn't explain, taking instead an image and emailing it to her. Her soft gasp in his earpiece let him know she'd received it. "What has hair that long? Be careful," she whispered.

"Aren't I always?"

"That's not reassuring," she snapped.

"Don't worry. I've got Doctor Manners here guarding my back."

What she said next made him bite his lip, especially when the doc's eyes widened. Jessie had quite the tongue on her – in and out of bed.

On silent feet, he continued on his way, following the trail of violence. Mason let out a low whistle as he popped from the dense trees into a clearing. "Holy cow."

"What? What is it?" Jessie's voice crackled in his ear, his Bluetooth not liking the reception out in the boonies.

"What kind of animal did you say Renee was?" he whispered as he held out a hand to hold back the doctor who also gaped at the scene.

"Fox. Why?"

"And how big are those?"

"I don't know, not big, like twenty to forty pounds, I think. Shifter ones tend to be larger of course. Mason, why are you asking me that? What's going on over there?"

He didn't answer. Couldn't, because he held his breath and froze in place. *Don't wake up. Don't wake up.* He silently chanted as he tried to take in the creature in the clearing.

Didn't work.

Immense eye lids pulled back to reveal an enormous pair of golden orbs. They were pretty compared to the giant fangs – longer than his arm – that emerged from a peeled lip.

"Mason," Jessie hissed. "Answer me. What's going on? Why is it so quiet?"

"Turns out Renee can shapeshift," he answered in a low rumble, not once taking his eyes off the massive red fox.

"That's good isn't it?" Jessie questioned.

"Not for me. She's freaking huge. I mean, she makes Miranda's bunny look cuddly."

"You're kidding."

"I wish," he muttered holding up his phone to take a picture. He sent it and a moment later his mate whistled.

"Damn, that's a big vixen. What are you going to do? And where's Viktor?"

Dr. Manners nudged him, then pointed. Underneath the giant, twitching tail, they caught a glimpse of a prone figure, naked and bloody, but Mason would recognize that close cropped haircut anywhere.

"Damn. That's him. He's not moving and I don't like the looks of that blood. Did she kill him?"

Manners shook his head. "I saw his chest moving. I think she's guarding him."

Taking a peek around at the wreckage of the camp, and the way the giant fox regarded them warily, her tail curled protectively around his friend, Mason agreed.

"So how do we get him out?"

"Why don't we ask?" Manners took a step forward. "Hi, Renee. Do you remember me? We met yesterday when you came in for some tests."

A growl, that just about shook the ground with its tenor, saw the doctor hastily retreat.

"Nice try, dumbass. Remind the girl of something she hates."

"What do you suggest then?" the doctor snapped.

"Don't you have like a tranquilizer, or sedative, or something?"

"Yeah, a bottle of them in my bag. Think she'll open wide so I can dump them in?" he asked sarcastically.

"Hey idiots," Jessie cajoled. "Why don't you wake up Viktor instead? I'll bet you if anyone can talk her into her human shape, it's him."

"I was just going to suggest that."

"Sure you were," Jessie agreed in a placating tone.

Worse, Mason could just picture her rolling her eyes in her office. Damn, but he loved her feathery ass. But she did make a good suggestion. "Viktor." Mason spoke in a loud whisper that made Renee's tail twitch. "Vi-i-k-t-o-r-r."

The enormous red fox tensed at his drawn out, sing song version of the name.

Dr. Manners snorted. "Keep going at it like that, and he'll sleep until next week and we'll end up dinner. This is how you do it. Quick, like a band aid. VIKTOR! WAKE UP!"

Up went the tail, back went the ears, and a mouthful of teeth appeared along with a low rumble that didn't bode well.

"Oh shit. Run!"

"Don't move," the doctor hissed. "If you run, she'll think you're prey."

Foot frozen in midair, Mason halted his planned escape and watched the bristling fox as she stood over his friend, her hackles up and teeth bared in a snarl. "So what should we do?"

"Nothing. I just saw Viktor move his hand which means he's regaining consciousness. We'll let him take care of his girlfriend."

"Good plan." Anything that involved Mason not getting eaten worked for him. But Mason had to wonder what was up with the guys he knew falling for women with great big fangs? First his brother and his saber

134

toothed bunny and now Viktor with his giant sized fox. He'd take his wife's normal sized feathery tail any day. Preferably bent over the armrest of the couch.

Chapter Seventeen

A deep growl, a tremble of the earth, and a face full of fur. "What the hell?" Viktor croaked as he came back to the land of the living, and a truckload of pain. A wet swipe of a tongue across his face had him sputtering. "Ew. Damn. What's going on?" Then a more pressing thought. "Renee!"

"Calm down, dude. Renee's fine, more or less."

Mason? What was the bear doing out here? On second thought, *why aren't I dead?* Last thing Viktor recalled, he got shot, more than once, and he told Renee to run. "Where is she?" He couldn't hide the panic in his tone.

"Right beside you," Mason replied. "She's the one licking your face."

Cracking open an eye and seeing the massive head hovering over him, big golden orbs staring intently, Viktor quickly understood she didn't flee as ordered. Instead, she'd stayed behind and saved his unworthy ass.

"Stubborn fox. I thought I told you to run," he growled.

She growled back. His lips curved into a smile. It seemed she'd not only found how to change into her beast, she'd also found some courage. He bared his teeth and chuckled when she snarled back at him.

"Um, Viktor, I don't think she's in her right mind at the moment. And given she could eat you as easily as the guys who captured you, you might want to think about staying on her good side."

"She wouldn't hurt me," he murmured, tangling his fingers in her fur, awed, despite himself, at her impressive stature. No wonder the mastermind wanted her. Short of a rare wooly mammoth he'd once seen as a boy, he'd never seen a shifter so big. Nor felt fur so soft. He tried to reach up a hand to stroke along her muzzle. Pain made him drop the attempt.

"Don't move," Dr. Manners admonished. "You're still bleeding from the holes in your body."

"No shit." Casting an irritated look at the doctor, Viktor restrained an urge to kill him. He didn't like people seeing him weak, especially not other predators. Mason, he made an exception for. They'd served overseas together – and he knew he could kick his ass in a fight. The doctor, however, was an unknown element. He looked harmless, but Viktor wondered what he hid behind his benign exterior.

"Hey, can you call your girlfriend off? She won't let us near you."

"Smart girl," he joked.

"She'll be a single girl if you don't let me take a look at you."

Renee single and available to the male population? Not while he had a breath left in his body. "Let the nice FUC agents check me out, Renee," he murmured.

She whined.

"It's okay. I trust them. So should you."

Backing away a few feet, she didn't once let her gaze stray from his body, or the two men that approached close enough to kneel by his side.

The doc wasted no time and pried his eyelids open and flashed them with a penlight. Viktor tolerated the checkup, only because he could see Renee watching warily, a low rumble shaking her.

"We need to get him back to the safe house or somewhere secure where I can set up a method of transfusion. He's lost a lot of blood."

Given his dizzy state, while lying down, Viktor couldn't disagree.

"Jessie's called in a medevac team. Says they'll be here in the next half hour," Mason said.

"What are we doing about Renee?" the doctor asked just as her ridiculously large tongue swiped Viktor again.

He fought not to giggle as it tickled. Croc's had more dignity than that. "What do you mean do about, Renee?" Viktor asked when their words penetrated.

"She won't fit on the chopper unless she swaps back."

"I'm more worried about her eating us when we try to move him. Have you seen the size of her teeth?" Mason exclaimed. "And I thought Miranda had the scariest set of fangs around."

As if hearing their comments, Renee lay down alongside Viktor, her head pillowed on her paws. The silky hairs on her side tickled his hand, and he moved his fingers enough that he could stroke her. "Watch what you say. You'll hurt her feelings, which, in turn, means I'll have to hurt you."

"Um, sorry, Renee. You have, um, really nice fur," Mason stammered.

Viktor snorted, but then flinched at the sharp pain in his chest. His vixen whined, then growled as the doctor swabbed one of the wounds on his chest.

"Um, Viktor, can you call her off."

"She won't hurt you."

"Just how many blows to the head did you take, anyway?" Mason asked.

"None. I just got shot a few times." He winced as the doctor, a wary eye on his vixen, applied pressure and bandages to the worst of his wounds. A stab of pain made him gasp, and Renee jumped to her feet, growling at the doc, hair hackled. "It's alright. He's just doing his job," Viktor hastened to say before she ate Dr. Manners. She let out a low whimper. "I know you're worried. It's going to take more than a few bullets," even big shotgun ones, "to keep me down. If you want to help, you need to change back."

She whined again.

"Can't remember how?"

The red vixen, hung her head.

He wanted to tell her not to worry. To just relax, but he coughed, a wet, nasty mess that started off a domino effect of pain and spurting blood. Then he couldn't say anything because the doctor poked him with something, and amidst a high pitched bark, Mason's shouts of alarm, and the tat-tat-tat of a helicopter approaching, darkness came to claim him.

*

Renee woke dressed in a clean gown, snuggled in a hospital bed alongside Viktor. Startled, because she possessed no recollection of getting there, she sat up with a gasp.

What happened? Last she remembered, men pointed weapons at them. They shot Viktor! Then nothing.

Obviously they'd survived, but how? Did they reside in the hands of the evil mastermind? Or did some good FUC's come to the rescue?

"We're safe."

Viktor's voice, gravelly and low, shifted her attention. She took in his wan face, his yellow slitted eyes laced with fatigue, and then noticed the bandages across his chest that the sheet didn't entirely cover.

She ran trembling fingers over the white expanse. "You were shot."

"Not the first time and probably not the last. I'll live. Thanks to you."

"Me? What did I do? I don't remember anything after I passed out. I'm such a wimp." She'd never win Viktor's heart if she kept fainting when he needed her. Viktor needed someone strong like him as a mate. And she so hoped she could be that woman. But once again, she got scared, and bam. She woke up after everything was done.

"You don't recall a thing?"

A shake of her head answered him.

He blew out a noisy sigh. "Damn. Where should I start then?"

"Who saved us?"

"You. Or, more accurately your fox did."

"I can't shift," she answered by rote.

"Oh yes you can. And mighty impressively, too. A lesser man would be intimidated, considering your fox is the size of a house."

"You're lying." She could see in his eyes he wasn't, though. "But how? Why now?"

"I suspect the great danger we were in triggered the change."

The danger to him, he should have said. Renee would have let anything happen to herself to save him. "What did I do after I changed?"

Uncertainty made his expression cloud. "Are you sure you want to know?

No! "Yes."

"From what the team gathered from the clues left behind, you shifted and then went ballistic on our captor's asses."

She gaped at him. "I killed them?"

"Yes."

The flicker in his eyes indicated he hid something. She just knew it. "What aren't you telling me?"

"I don't know if I should tell you."

"Tell me. I have a right to know." How bad could it be?

"You didn't just kill the bad guys, Renee, you ate them. Or most of them anyway. The FUC team did find a few stray bits."

A hard swallow was all she could manage as she digested the bit of info. *I shapeshifted into a giant fox and then ate the enemy?* That was so, so... "Awesome!" And perhaps explained why her mouth tasted like she'd eaten one of Viktor's rare steaks. She'd have to remember to floss.

"Why awesome?" His brow creased.

Hopping off the bed, she fist pumped the air. "I kicked butt. Took no prisoners. I finally stood up for myself." Her smile drooped. "I wish I could remember." It would have rocked to remember what courage felt like. But hey, the important part was knowing the bravery existed inside her. It just needed the right conditions to come out.

"Um, well, while we didn't catch the actual fight, Mason did take pictures of your beast. I can have him show them to you if you'd like."

"Would I ever!" Maybe now that she knew for sure morphing was possible, she'd have an easier time trying to do it. "So, we're in the hands of the good guys?"

"Yes. Annoying FUC ones who won't let me go home to sleep in my own bed."

"How did we get here?"

141

"Helicopter."

"Me too?"

"Yup. Although Dr. Manners had to threaten you first with leaving you behind when you wouldn't change back. Once your fox realized we were serious, you swapped shapes and swooned like a girl."

"Did not."

"Did too, right on top of me, thank you very much."

She winced. "Sorry?"

"I'll live."

Crawling back on the bed, she tucked the blanket up around him. "You're still injured."

"Healing," he corrected. "And I'd heal much faster if they let me leave."

"You were shot. You need to rest."

"When did you get your doctor's degree?" he snapped. But she didn't take offence. She knew Viktor well enough to understand he didn't appreciate appearing weak in front of her.

"You're grouchy when you're hurt. Lucky for you, I can handle it. Whether you like it or not, I'm not letting you out of this bed," she announced.

"You're bossy," he grumbled, but she could hear the affection in his tone.

"Concerned," she corrected, snuggling against him. Chagrin made her bite her lip at his sudden stillness. She'd inadvertently hurt him, not that the stubborn man would admit it.

"I'd prefer you be concerned back at my place. Then at least I could order you to get naked and serve me some food."

"Are you hungry?" she asked, sitting up and peeking around for something to feed him.

"Oh, I'm hungry alright. Come here."

142

Snagging his fingers in her hair, he turned her head and brought it down, devouring her lips like a man starving. Despite her meal of enemy shifters, she embraced him back just as eagerly. Sucking his bottom lip. Stroking his tongue with her own, until someone cleared their voice.

"Ahem."

Viktor didn't let her go, and she sighed happily in his mouth. She didn't want to stop either.

"Sorry to interrupt Agent Smith, but – well, that's just rude."

Renee opened her eyes to see Viktor's middle finger up and wagging at the doctor. She pulled away, cheeks heating.

"Hello, Dr. Manners."

"Renee. Nice to see you smiling instead of snarling. You seem no worse for wear."

"Have you come to set me free?" Viktor snapped.

"Not exactly. You're not even close to healed. But, we thought you and Renee might want to sit in on a meeting we're having about the mastermind, especially seeing as how he was behind the attempt to kidnap you both."

A hard glint entered Viktor's eyes. "I wouldn't miss it."

"Vic-c-t-tor!" Miranda's yell bounced into the room before she did. "Are you alright? I heard you got taken with your pants down by some dirty coons. Oh hi, Renee." Miranda paused in her loud exclamation to wave and smile.

Renee waved back as Viktor sighed.

Miranda ignored him. "Hey Renee, I hear your fox kicked some major bad guy ass. Awesome."

"Thanks." Renee, while not recalling the event in question, still blushed at the praise.

"Poor Victor. Once again, a girl saves your ass." Miranda smirked.

Viktor growled and his eyes narrowed.

Despite her liking for the bunny, Renee didn't appreciate anyone upsetting her croc, especially since he recovered from wounds earned while trying to save her. "Viktor would have saved me if he'd not gotten hit with sedatives, locked in a cage, then shot."

Miranda didn't give him a break. "You're getting old, Victor."

Renee slid off the bed and put her hands on her hips. "Why do you keep calling him Victor? His name is Viktor."

"Is not."

"Is too."

"Is not."

"Actually it is," Viktor interjected.

"Figures. Take her side instead of your partner's." Miranda beamed. "About time you fell in love."

Renee's jaw dropped at Miranda's conclusion. *Could he possibly love me?* Surely not. But despite her disbelief, warmth spread through her, along with doubt as she waited for his reply.

*

"Love? No – it's complicated." Viktor cheeks heated – for the first time ever – as he stuttered trying to explain how his actions didn't mean he loved Renee.

Not that Miranda listened, or cared as she bounced around singing, "Viktor and Renee, sitting in a tree, k-i-s-s-i-n-g."

Then he didn't bother trying to clarify because his foxy lady beamed, and blushed. How could he lie and say what he felt was less than love? Wait a second. He loved her? Shit. When had that happened?

Sure he liked Renee – a lot. But still, it didn't mean he'd succumbed to Cupid's curse.

What else to call his feelings for her, though? If analyzed, he'd have to admit he more than just liked her. He didn't like anyone touching her. Or looking at her. Or possibly thinking about her.

But still, jealousy didn't equal love.

What about the fact he needed her with him at all times? He could lie and claim it was so he could properly protect her. Not because the moments spent apart sucked, or because he enjoyed the way she touched him without fear, and smiled at him.

Sigh. Deny it all he wanted, it circled back to one conclusion. He loved her.

In the middle of her song, Miranda was yanked out of the room by a hairy arm accompanied by a gruff, "Sorry. She got away from me. I'll see you at the meeting." Chase to the rescue.

"Ah yes, the meeting." Doctor Manners, who'd ignored the impromptu floor show while checking Viktor's vitals, straightened. "Kloe's arranged for it to happen here at the safe house so you wouldn't have to travel far to attend. If you'll just follow me, we should get going, unless you want me to fetch the wheelchair."

Viktor made a menacing sound.

"Walking it is."

Swinging his legs out of bed, Viktor grimaced down at the robe he wore. Then scowled as Renee, wearing the same gown, presented him her back and through the gaps in the hospital wear, her very naked backside.

"We need some clothes." Because no way was he flashing his ass to the world and he most definitely didn't want anyone else seeing hers. Unless they didn't mind dying.

Dr. Manners pulled out some standard sweats, the grey pants and shirts swimming on Renee's more slender frame and stretching on his.

Lacing his fingers through hers – the scowl on his face daring anyone to comment – they followed the doc to the meeting room ensconced in the center of the safe house. Entering the pale, yellow walled room filled with a long scarred wooden table surround by chairs, he took quick stock of the occupants; Miranda – wearing a bright smile – Chase –with his perpetual glower – Jessie – head down as she typed on her tablet – Mason – wearing his habitual smirk – and of course, Kloe, who just looked frazzled.

The doctor closed the door after they entered and leaned against it. Easing himself into a chair, Viktor held onto Renee's hand as she slid into the seat beside him.

Kloe clapped her hands for attention. "Now that everyone is here, let's get started. As you all know, the mastermind is not dead as we hoped, but still very much active as evidenced by the attempted kidnapping of agent Smith and his charge, Renee. Thanks to the emergence of Renee's fox side, they managed to escape."

Viktor couldn't help but cringe at the stark relaying of his failure. But, if he looked at the positive, at least Renee found her beast.

Miranda held up her hand and waved it.

"Yes Miranda."

"Given Renee's awesome handling of the minions, I say we give her honorary FUC agent status."

A chorus of ayes met her suggestion, and Viktor squeezed Renee's hand, his heart tight at the look of astonishment on her face.

"But I don't even remember doing anything," his vixen exclaimed.

"So? The important thing is you kept yourself and Victor alive."

"And you didn't eat me," Mason added. "For which my wife is very thankful."

Jessie flipped her dark hair tipped in white. "Oh please. As if anyone would voluntarily eat any part of your tough body." Jessie no sooner spoke, than she slapped a hand over her mouth. The color in her cheeks just increased the treble of the snickers going around the table.

"Ahem." Kloe's stern gaze stifled the mirth. "Since we all agree, congratulations Renee. You've been officially FUC'd."

Renee choked while the laughter in the room ran wild, to the point even Viktor stifled a grin. Kloe, looking pleased with herself, chortled along with everyone else.

Slapping the table, Kloe called for order again. "Now that we've gotten that out of the way, let's get back to the mastermind. I find it disturbing that he knew where to find agent Smith and Renee. Jessie, any idea on how that happened? I thought you'd firewalled our computers against invasion after the last attack."

"I did."

"Then how did the mastermind find out? Only a select few knew of Viktor's plans," Kloe said.

"Not only did barely anyone know, we never put to paper, or inputted to the computer their plan to go."

"But," Mason interjected, "they did discuss it with Dr. Manners before they left."

Viktor wasn't the only one who turned a hard stare the doctor's way.

"It's not him," Miranda scoffed. "My mom knows his. Nolan's as clean as they come."

"I can assure you, I would never resort to working for someone as sick as the mastermind. If I were to plot evil, I would run the show." The doctor grinned while Kloe rolled her eyes.

"If we trust that those Viktor told aren't working for the criminal, that leaves us with only one possibility," Mason said.

"A spy!" Miranda hopped up. "I say we ferret the sucker out, let Viktor at him, or her, and find out what they know."

"Why does Viktor get to torture the culprit? I think we should draw straws," Mason said with a pout.

"Or arm wrestle," Chase added, around a mouthful of honeybun.

"Shouldn't we first find the informant before we call dibs on questioning?" Kloe remarked dryly.

"I can tell you where the spy is," Jessie announced, looking up from her tablet screen.

"You can? Don't stop now. Tell us where."

"The spy is right here in the safe house. I show several calls leaving the building and going to some pay as you go cell phones that are now dead. Given the screening all the staff and guards went through to work in here, that leaves the victims we rescued from the lab. One of them must have overhead Viktor's plans with Renee, alerted the mastermind, who then sent those hunters after them."

"How does he keep getting past our defenses?" Mason grumbled.

"Why do you keep saying 'he'?" Renee asked, forehead creased.

Viktor froze. "Do you know something we don't, Renee?"

"I guess I should have said something before, but I was afraid the mastermind would hurt me if she found out. Mastermind is a woman. And not a very nice one."

A fly fart would have sounded loud in the silence following her announcement.

"A woman? Why didn't you say something before?" Kloe's quiet question started a barrage.

Questions hammered Renee from every side, and before she could duck under the table to hide, Viktor hauled her onto his lap and pressed her head into his shoulder. Then he roared. "Enough!"

"But…"

"Would you like to discuss this with me outside?" Viktor growled.

"Um, no." Mason sat back down and feigned interest in the ceiling.

"A shame. My freezer needed stocking. As for the fact the mastermind is a woman, yes, it's a shock. But don't go blaming Renee. None of us questioned her. None of us thought to, not even me, seeing as how nobody ever seemed to recall anything. Not even her closest minions."

"I should have told you, though," Renee admitted softly.

"Why didn't you?" he asked, in a gentle tone that contrasted sharply with the one he used on the rest of the room.

"Mastermind doesn't know I remember her. No one knows. I was scared she'd find out. People who know what she looks like have a tendency to disappear. Except for Gregory and one of the scientists. They were the only ones allowed to recall her. Everyone else took the special pills and forgot."

"But given your resistance to drugs, she must have guessed you were immune?"

Renee shrugged. "I heard her talking about it with Gregory one time when I was pretending to sleep. She thought because she'd brainwashed me before my accident, that it stuck."

"Can you tell us what she looks like?"

"She's easy to spot. She's really short. Kind of stocky with prominent front teeth. Brown hair to her shoulders. Really thick glasses."

"A woman with glasses?" Mason said with disgust. "Now how am I supposed to punch the mastermind's lights out?"

"Easy. I'll do it for you," Jessie announced, flipping her hair back in a ruffle.

A groan escaped the doctor. "Oh shit. Short with glasses? We don't have a spy. The mastermind is one of the victims in the safe house."

"You're kidding?" Viktor didn't know if he should be elated or freaked that the enemy they'd searched for resided so close by.

"Oh, that's bad," Renee said. "I hope you don't have computers here. She's really good with them."

Renee no sooner finished speaking than the lights went out and they all heard an ominous click. The windowless space turned pitch black except for the glow of Jessie's tablet screen and no back up lights flicked on. It seemed the mastermind planned her attack well.

"What's happening?" Viktor asked.

"The safe house has gone into lockdown mode," Dr. Manners announced.

"Jessie, can you reverse it?" Kloe asked.

Tapping madly on her tablet, not affected by the power outage, Jessie mumbled under her breath. "I don't believe it. The four eyed bitch activated the lockdown in this section only."

"So undo it," Mason replied.

"I'm working on it, but she also managed to change the safe house security code, which I now need to decode. This could take a little while."

Too long, in other words, Viktor thought, to capture the slippery criminal. She'd one upped them once again. But, at least now, they had a face – and the proper sex – to go with the evil monster. And stuck in here, with him, Renee was safe.

But once they left, who knew when the mastermind would come after her again. *Let her, because I'll be waiting and I won't show mercy, woman or not.*

Chapter Eighteen

Muahahahaha.

Mastermind laughed her little ass off as she locked all her nemesis in one location. She knew she couldn't keep hiding amongst them forever, and actually looked forward to leaving the boring safe house. The only thing she regretted was not being able to get her revenge on the FUC agents who kept spoiling her plots. But then again, perhaps she should thank them, because their intervention finally gave her the answer she needed. The secret to becoming a predator such as the world had never known.

Forget clinical trials. Forget hiding in the shadows. She was ready for the final step in her transformation.

The needle sank in with the lovely concoction the good doctor created to combat the experimentation, a slightly tweaked version of course. After the mishap with the one armed failure, she'd revised her initial dosage and now couldn't wait to taste success – and the blood of those who stood in her way.

Mastermind waited for the potion to take effect. Drummed her fingers knowing she couldn't wait too long as Jessie had probably already contacted outside help. Dratted swan and her technical skills. What a shame she insisted on working for FUC.

Impatient, the mastermind loaded some more syringes with her special cocktail and then flitted about the ward with its snoring occupants, injecting her failures, cackling as she bestowed the gift of greatness – in smaller doses of course, as she intended to be strongest of them all.

Some of the recipients woke with gasps. Others, hearing her maniacal laughter, huddled and cried. She left none of them untouched.

Done, she jumped onto a supply cart, lost her balance and fell as it rolled. Once back to her feet, she climbed on a chair and stood.

"Monstrous creations," she orated, her squeaky voice still not attaining the proper treble to inspire fear. "It is I, Mastermind."

Only a few of the experiments bothered to pay her any mind. This wouldn't do at all.

"I command you to listen." She stamped a tiny foot.

"You're the mastermind?" The snorted query raised her ire.

"Someone has visions of grandeur, or should I say shorture." Laughter met the insult.

The mockery wasn't acceptable. "Do not make fun of me."

"What are you going to do about it?" The amphibian, who could no longer regain his human shape, rose from his bed. "You don't have the drugs you used to subdue us. You don't have your minions. Actually, you have nothing to use against us."

Okay, this wasn't how she'd planned her grand return. Apparently, the mastermind had done her job of making them forget a little too well. They didn't have any respect for her intellect or evil nature. She'd show them. "I shall use my enhanced beast and you will tremble before my greatness." Except, her beast wouldn't come. Eyes squinched tight, fists clenched, whole body ready to burst, nothing happened. Not a single claw or hair sprouted.

153

And the laughter, started by one frog who now topped the list of people she intended to kill, cascaded into a wave. Worse, the ungrateful wretches left their beds and joined the frog in advancing on her, menace in their eyes.

But the mastermind wasn't about to become their ball in the game of keep away. Darting as fast as her little legs could go, she fled, sliding through the legs of the tall creature the scientists jokingly called Sasquatch into the hall. She hurriedly tapped the code to lock the room.

Outside, she heard the thump of fist hitting the main door as the arriving reinforcements discovered the door code changed. She didn't have long before they broke in and without her expected army of minions – ungrateful wretches who wouldn't obey – she decided it less than prudent to stay. Forgetting plan B, and C, both of which involved her shifting into a creature more daunting than Godzilla, she skipped right down to plan H.

They never even thought to look in the ducts ventilating the place. Idiots.

And once again, I prove I am smarter than them.

Muahahahaha. Now if only she could figure out why her serum didn't work, and why she suddenly had a craving for cheese enchiladas.

Chapter Nineteen

Jessie cracked the code for the lockdown just as agents broke down the door to the safe house. As they poured out of their temporary jail, reinforcements swept the building. But while all the patients were accounted for – if overly excited – of Mastermind there wasn't a sign.

The wily villain escaped again.

Given the breach in security, Nolan, who insisted they drop the Dr. Manners title while they sat in the dark twiddling their thumbs, allowed Viktor to go home – along with a posse of FUC guards – with the instructions to not indulge in strenuous activity.

As if.

Ensconced in his apartment, guards outside the door, with his own version of a lockdown in effect – meaning nothing short of a bomb would get someone in to his place – he stripped as he headed for his bathroom.

"What are you doing?" Renee asked, her query a touch breathless.

"Showering? Are you coming with me?" And he meant *come*.

Quicker than he could reload a weapon, she stood naked before him. Oh yeah, he loved his fox. Although what he'd do about it remained to be seen. Could he make room for her in his life? Did he have what it took to keep a fox happy? Was it time to take a mate?

For once, he didn't have the answers and killing wouldn't solve the problem. All he knew was he loved her, and for now, he'd just leave it at that.

As he heated up the shower, much warmer than he usually took in deference to her mammal state, he drew her into his arms, the tension in his body fading. *She's safe.* The entire ride home, he'd watched like a hawk for signs of being followed. Viktor even allowed Mason to check out his place for signs of an intruder before he kicked him out.

Alone, with Renee, surrounded by enough guns and ammo to kill even the most armored of villains, and in need of some healing, the sexual kind, Viktor didn't bother to fight his desire.

He wanted Renee. Needed her. Loved her. And dammit all, he was going to have her, in a bed this time. No hunters, no evil criminal out to get them, no smirking coworkers. Just him and his fox.

Naked, hot water cascaded over them as he luxuriated in the sensation of her smooth skin pressed against his. Their lips met in a soft clash of teeth as they both eagerly sought to control the embrace.

Forget his injuries. The bandages got wet, and he didn't care. She was the only cure for what pained him.

Leaving her lips, he buried his face against her neck, the flutter of her pulse against his lips. Oh how her slick skin proved an oral delight. He nibbled his way lower, but gasped when he attempted to crouch, the gunshot to his thigh too tender for the position. Standing back up, he threaded his fingers in her damp hair and rested his forehead against hers.

"I'm sorry."

"For what? Being injured and trying to do exactly the opposite of what the doctor ordered?"

A wry grin curved his lips. "He told me to eat and get my strength up."

"I somehow doubt that was the meal he had in mind," she teased, grasping his innuendo.

"But it's the one I intend to enjoy once we're done in here and get to the bed."

"Or, you could let me have a turn."

Before his brain could process what she meant, she dropped to her knees and put herself eye to eye with his cock. Swamp help him. Just knowing what she planned made his dick twitch. She licked him and all coherence left his head, along with the blood. But he'd never been happier to be stupid than at that moment when she wrapped her lips around him.

*

Renee wasn't exactly sure if she did it right, but taking the advice of Miranda, who whispered instructions in her ear before they left the safe house on how to deal with Viktor's stress, Renee took a hold of Viktor's shaft and proceeded to explore it. Using her lips and mouth, tongue, and even the edge of her teeth, she sucked the hard length of him. Tasted the soft skin covering his erratic pulse. Grazed the tip of him with her teeth. Licked the salty pearl that emerged. And she enjoyed every minute of it.

Judging by his groans, rigid stance, and closed eyes, Viktor enjoyed it too. It made her insanely happy. When they'd come together previously, he'd feasted on her and she wondered after – because in the throes all she could do was feel – how he enjoyed caressing such an intimate part of her. Now, roles reversed, in charge of his bliss and succeeding, she enjoyed the heady and erotic power of having him react to her touch. Of having him vulnerable to her caress. *Of being mine.*

She could have sucked him all evening. Wanted to see how he'd taste when he gave in to the pleasure completely.

"Renee," he whispered her name, reverently.

A moan of pleasure rumbled through her body as she eagerly bobbed.

"Look at me," he ordered.

She peeked up and saw him, eyes hooded with passion, intense and so handsome, a quiver went through her.

"Bend over for me."

She ignored his request to swirl her tongue around the tip of him.

He sucked in a breath, then chuckled. "And to think I called you innocent. You learn quickly. And while I would love to finish in your mouth, I don't think I have the strength to go another round. Not today at any rate, and I refuse to leave you hanging. So bend over for me."

With a grumble of regret, she popped him free of her mouth, then stood to face him. He took her mouth hard, demanding. She moaned as their tongues danced, then moaned again as his fingers slid between their bodies and he played with her clit.

Already hot and ready for him, she swayed into his touch, aching for him. He manipulated her so that she faced away, then bent her over, with a gruff order to, "Brace yourself."

Hands flat against the shower wall, she caught her breath when he rubbed the tip of his shaft against her sex. Slick for him, he slid back and forth with ease against her, the friction on her clit making her hips twitch back, looking for more.

"You are so perfect," he murmured. He eased into her, a decadent inch at a time, stretching her, filling her. He went so slow, she wanted to scream. Instead, she pushed back against him, her buttocks abutting up against his thighs and burying his cock as far as it could go.

Her channel pulsed around him, and he growled as his fingers dug into her hips. "Impatient vixen."

158

"Decisive," she corrected. "I know what I want. I want you."

"I'm yours," he answered in a gruff whisper. He withdrew then thrust, jolting a cry from her. Again, in and out, he pumped. Stroked. Took her with a gentle passion that built her erotic tension.

"Come for me," he demanded in a low voice, tight with need. He slid a hand from her hip and curled it under her body, finding and stroking her nub. The intense sensation made her gasp. Her channel clenched. Rippled. His cock answered by swelling further as he continued to grind against her, deep and hard.

She came with drawn out scream, her whole body coming apart at his hands and cock. He murmured his pleasure, and joined her with a shout of her name and a final thrust that spilled his seed, hot and welcome inside.

Limp, she would have slumped to the shower floor, but somehow, he pulled her upright and into the spray. He washed her with gentle hands, his eyes tender, and in that moment, Renee realized she was in love. In love with the fierce croc who turned into the most caring of men for her alone.

She didn't announce her revelation fearing she'd scare him off, or that he'd try and refute her emotions. But as she lay cradled in his arms, bodies snuggled skin to skin, she was determined to do everything she could to keep him and show him that she had what it took to be his mate.

I'll do anything to make this moment last forever. Anything to have him love me.

Chapter Twenty

Viktor woke in a great mood. It could have had something to do with the fact a vixen lay curled against him. Or that his injuries were mostly healed and barely twinged when he stretched. And the sun was shining. Okay, who was he kidding? It had everything to do with Renee.

Something about her, everything in fact, drew him despite all logic. He could list a number of reasons why they shouldn't stay together. But his one reason for keeping her, *I love her,* eradicated all the excuses not to. And perhaps it was presumptuous of him, but he hoped she felt the same way. She certainly seemed to with the way she was at ease only around him. How, despite the fact she'd mostly overcome her fear of the sky, she still insisted on holding onto him.

Driven into work by a FUC agent after a leisurely breakfast – where he put his counter to good use and exercised his tongue – he ignored the chauffeur's amusement to tug Renee onto his lap. He nuzzled her neck, loving the rattling sound of pleasure she made. He was a changed man, around her at any rate. He'd once made fun of men who lost their dignity for love. Now, he couldn't imagine life any other way. And he dared anyone to make fun of him. He could use some new targets for practice.

Happy, yet still pessimistic, he couldn't help but wonder what would happen to ruin what he and Renee had together. Would the mastermind come after Renee?

Viktor didn't have any qualms about taking the bitch down, glasses wearing girl or not. Nobody hurt his vixen.

However, the danger to his newfound happiness didn't end up coming in the package he expected. Nor was it one he could fight.

Entering the FUC offices, agents shouting out congratulations and teasing remarks about getting his ass saved by a girl, Renee alternated between beaming at the praise and scowling at the jokes.

"Why do they keep laughing? Don't they understand you were shot?" she grumbled. "You would have saved me otherwise."

Viktor shrugged, amused at her irritation on his behalf. "It's what friends do. They joke about things we don't find funny. Don't worry. We'll get our chance to do the same back at some point." Or he'd get them on the training grounds when he worked the agents extra hard. Hide behind his girlfriend indeed!

The receptionist smiled as she saw them. "Good morning, you two. Good job on kicking those hunters asses, Renee. You just proved once again why women are needed for a better FUC. And Viktor, glad to see you're recovering."

He grumbled in reply.

Undaunted, the blonde behind the desk, grinned wider. "Kloe's waiting in her office with a surprise."

"What surprise?"

"You'll both see."

With that enigmatic reply, the receptionist ignored them to answer the phone.

"What could it be?" Renee asked.

"I don't know, but I say we find out." But he couldn't shake the trepidation attempting to dig its claws in. In the heart of the FUC office, he didn't fear danger, but a knot in his gut told him to pick Renee up and run.

As soon as he walked into his boss's office, he silently cursed and wished he'd followed his instincts. Especially when he saw the alligator skin bag.

*

Viktor paused mid-step and Renee bumped into his back. What caused him to hesitate?

He didn't say a word as he stepped aside and tugged Renee forward. Before she could ask him what was wrong, a large woman with fire-engine-red hair, enveloped her in a hug surely meant to crush every bone in her body. "Mon bébé! Oh que je t'ai manqué, ma petite."

Renee panicked. Pushing at the hugging woman, she scrambled away and hid behind Viktor, wrapping her arms around his waist. Her heart raced as her mind tried to tell her why the woman looked familiar. She hid from the truth instead, burying her face in his back.

"Why does she hide?" asked the stranger with a strong accent.

"She doesn't do well with surprises," Viktor explained. "Perhaps if you told her who you are."

Why would introductions matter? Renee still wouldn't want a stranger to strangle her.

"Moi? I am Madame Louise Renarde, her mother."

A good thing Renee held on to Viktor because her knees went weak at the announcement. Peeking around his side, she looked at the woman who made the declaration. Almost as tall as Renee, with brighter brassy locks, familiar golden orbs and a smell... Renee inhaled a scent which seemed hauntingly familiar. Could this woman truly be her mother?

Kloe confirmed it. "Sorry to spring the surprise on you, but she arrived just this morning from Quebec,

Canada. As per Viktor's request, we sent out a notice to all the FUC offices seeing if we could match up Renee with any of the missing children reports."

"Renee? Who is Renee?" asked the woman. "My bébé's name is Monique. Monique Renarde of the Montreal Red Fox Clan."

"We gave her a name when we rescued her because she couldn't recall her own," Kloe answered as Renee tried to digest the news.

My mother. Monique. The startling revelations spun in her mind and Renee didn't know what to do, or say. She didn't find help from her croc. Viktor stood still as a statue, not speaking. She hugged him, but he didn't offer the expected reassurance.

"I thank the FUC agents for rescuing her, *finally.*" The hard emphasis eloquently stated what Louise Renarde thought of the timeframe. "But now, if you'll excuse us, my daughter and I have much to catch up on. I will book us a flight home as soon as possible."

Viktor finally spoke. "She's still in danger. The mastermind is out there and possibly looking for a way to get her back."

"Then perhaps you should do your job and hunt this criminal instead of seducing my daughter."

Renee's eyes widened as her mother guessed – correctly – at their relationship.

"I care a great deal for Ren–Monique," Viktor stated, although the way he said it, in a flat monotone, sounded anything but.

"Cared so much you didn't pay attention and they almost caught her? I hear she is the one who rescued you both from some villains. It seems to me perhaps she is not the one who needs protecting. Non?"

Renee didn't like the implication and stepped forth from behind Viktor, ready to defend him.

"Viktor did his best, but we were ambushed."

"His best almost saw you lost again."

Taking a deep breath, she didn't hide from the woman who spoke so sharply, but Renee stood her ground, protecting her croc. "It was an unfortunate incident that, thankfully, turned out well. I don't want you talking bad about him. He's been nothing but good to me."

To Renee's horror – *or should I be calling myself Monique now?* – her mother burst into tears. "Oh, mon dieu. I waited so long to find you, only to have you take the side of this - this lizard. How your ancestors must be turning in their graves." Her mother wailed and Renee/Monique could only gape in horror. What should she do? Somehow her first impulse to run didn't seem appropriate.

"I think I should leave," Viktor said softly.

Panicked, Renee – because the name Monique just didn't feel right – turned to grip his shirt. "No. Don't go. Please. I need you."

Eyes and expression blank, he brushed a strand of hair back from her face. "Your mother has missed you. She's your family. Go. Spend some time with her. I won't be far if you need me."

When he would have left without even a kiss, Renee flung her arms around him and forced one upon his lips. Stiff at first, his mouth softened under her frantic embrace. He broke it off and leaned his forehead against hers, whispering, "Everything will be alright."

Then he left, and an ache took up residence in her heart. Why did it feel like goodbye?

*

Viktor wanted to hit something. Wanted to grab Renee and run. Wanted to…have the impossible.

Faced with the fact Renee belonged to a family, had roots and a life, which though forgotten, waited for her to return, made him realize how foolish his dream was.

I should have known better than to think a cold blooded croc could keep his sweet fox. It wasn't just age that separated them, but genesis. She belonged with her family and others of her kind. While some species could interbreed, cold and hot couldn't. He could never give Renee what she deserved – children, a family of her own.

While she might protest his decision now, he did it for her own good, and in time, she'd accept it. No matter how it crushed his finally beating heart.

The biggest question was, how to leave the scene gracefully? Did he do the honorable thing and tell her upfront things were over? Or should he disappear into the swamp until she left and forgot about him?

His mind said he should choose honesty. The ache in his heart, though, won. He couldn't tell her to go. Couldn't tell her to leave him and not look back. He wanted Renee. Wanted her forever, even if he wasn't the best thing for her. Even if she deserved better. He loved her too much to set her free.

So, for the first time in his life, he chose the cowardly route. He faded into the background as Kloe handled the reunion. Shadowed them when the trio went to lunch. He didn't do it just because of his promise to Renee to stay nearby. He worried the mastermind would resurface. Yes, his vixen's beast was big and dangerous, but as he'd learned, she couldn't call upon it at will.

Hidden, and out of touch, he would watch over her, until he knew she was safe. No matter how long it took. And then, he'd retire to the swamp. Become an ornery croc for real, like his uncle Boris, remembering and regretting the times of warmth, the times he held her in his arms.

Damn his sappy thoughts. Where was an enemy when he needed to maim something?

Chapter Twenty One

After Viktor left her to the mercy of her mother, who alternated between ranting at the injustice of Renee's captivity in a mixture of French and English, and the sobs of how much she missed her, Renee vacillated between fascination in discovering the past she'd forgotten, and unease. She'd not liked the way she and her croc parted. Something about his kiss and words screamed he wasn't coming back. But surely he wouldn't leave her, not after what they shared?

Hours later, fed, her mind full of stories and details about the life she used to have, Renee was ready to go home. Home to her croc. A part of her understood the woman she'd spent the day with was her mother, something she'd always wanted. But, she couldn't remember her. Couldn't remember any of the people she spoke of, or the stories she related. Didn't feel the instant bond and sense of coming home like she had when she met Viktor. She needed to see him.

"When is Viktor coming to get me?" Renee asked as her mother bustled around the small kitchen within the rented hotel suite. Human owned, Kloe wasn't pleased with the choice, stating they wouldn't have the ability to protect them as well. Louise Renarde, though, did as she chose.

"He is not returning."

Renee's heart stalled, but she didn't think it had anything to do with the drugs she used to take. "What do you mean he's not coming back?"

167

Placing the Chinese take-out they'd purchased before coming upstairs onto plates, her mother paused. "I don't want that man coming near you. That dirty lizard has taken enough advantage."

"Don't talk about him like that. He loves me. And I love him."

"He has told you that?"

"No, but –"

Mother's lip curled. "Pfft! You can do much better than an animal that lives in muddy water. When we return to Quebec, I will introduce you to some proper men. Like Francois, the son of some friends of mine. He is from a very distinguished family of silver foxes."

Leave? "But I don't want to go to Quebec. I want to stay here." *With Viktor.*

"Stay here for what? There is nothing here for you."

"Viktor's here."

"Is he?" her mother replied slyly.

True, Renee had not seen him since the morning, but he'd promised to stay nearby. He would have kept his word. "I know he's not far. He's my protector."

"My poor bébé. I fear you are mistaken. He is done with you. There is no reason to stay. He has done what most men do –conquered your pants and moved on to his next conquest."

"He wouldn't do that. He cares for me," Renee said, refusing to give in to her headstrong mother. As if she'd believe a stranger when her own instincts screamed that the man she'd gotten to know wouldn't use her that way. He'd fought his attraction to her and lost because he felt something, something more than just a carnal need.

"Cares for you? I doubt that. I heard the story of your courtship, or lack of. He tried to have you assigned to someone else."

"Because he was being honorable. I made him keep me."

"And did you make him seduce you too?"

Her red cheeks answered that question.

"Mon dieu. Non. Ce n'est pas acceptable. You will forget this man and come home where you belong."

"No, I'm not." When her mother would have spoken again, Renee held up a hand. "No. You need to listen to me. While I am delighted I found you and I've always wanted a mother, I don't remember you. Or the life we had before the lab. I want to learn about my roots. Get to know you, but I'm not going to give up the one thing, the one person who makes life finally worth living. I want to get to know you and have you in my life, but you have to understand, I need him. I love him."

"Too late. The arrangements have been made. You will come back with me, home where you belong. You will forget this crocodile. As if that would work. Don't you know, our kind can't mate with theirs?"

Renee pressed her lips together. "If you were hoping for grandchildren, then you're out of luck. I've imbibed so many drug cocktails and had my ovaries harvested so many times, there isn't a darned egg left. Or none that would prove viable." A sad fact she'd had years to come to terms with. Beside, having spent so much time incarcerated, she wanted time to live, to love, to discover. She'd leave children to those less damaged both in body and spirit. Her, she wanted adventure, and her croc.

Her announcement of her sterility finally silenced her mother. Renee waited for her to go off on another tangent, or start crying again, but got a surprise.

"My poor bébé. You've had such a hard life."

"Yes I have, which is why I'm determined to hold on to the happiness I've found." She'd hold on to it like the most stubborn of foxes.

"And you think this lizard is the answer?"

Renee smiled. "I know you think he brainwashed me, and it's funny, because he was also very concerned about taking advantage of me. But what you both need to understand is I've met lots of men while incarcerated. The scientists even tried to pair me up with other prisoners before they realized I couldn't reproduce. None of them ever affected me like he does. I love him."

"I'm not handling this very well, am I?" A heavy sigh left her mother, a woman who wanted back the little girl she lost, but instead got a frightened, damaged woman who wasn't quite sure how to handle the situation.

Renee shrugged. "I don't know if there is a proper way. But even though I want to stay here with Viktor, I do want to get to know you. I've always wondered about my mother."

"Then what my girl wants, she gets. I guess if you are serious about this lizard I shall have to get rid of my alligator leather, handcrafted purses."

"Mother!"

A grin spread across her mother's face. "And now I see your father in you. He would be so proud of you for surviving and not letting the mastermind win."

Renee felt a pang of sadness at never having known the man who died within a few years of her kidnapping. Just one of many things she'd learned over the course of the day. "Thanks."

This time when they hugged, Renee didn't run away, and for just a moment, she remembered what it was like to be a little girl again, loved by her mother.

Chapter Twenty Two

Staked outside the hotel where Renee and her mother stayed, Viktor slumped in his seat. He elected to remain out of sight, taking up position in a van parked in the alley instead of stationed near Madame Renarde's room. He didn't want Renee's feelings for him to interfere with her reunion with her mother. But dammit it all, he hated it.

He wanted to give her a shoulder to lean on if things got tough. Wanted to hold her hand and give her the reassurance she probably needed.

Why did doing the right thing have to suck?

The passenger door opened and he aimed his gun at a forehead before he'd even blinked. He eased off the trigger when he recognized Mason.

"What are you doing out here moping?" the bear asked as he clambered in, rocking the van.

"I don't mope. I skulk."

Mason snickered. "Sure, you are. Is that what they call hiding in an alley? I never knew crocs had yellow bellies."

Bristling, Viktor snarled, "Are you calling me a coward? I never back down from a fight."

"Until now."

A forearm against his friend's throat shut Mason up as Viktor growled. "I am not a coward."

Mason gurgled, so he eased up on the pressure. "Touchy. Touchy. But seriously, what the hell do you call sitting out here *skulking* while the woman you love is up there with her long lost mother making plans to leave?"

"It's what's best for her."

The choking sound coming from his friend had nothing to do with Viktor, who'd slumped back in his seat.

Mason continued to snort. "I can't believe you just said that. How is sending her back home, heartbroken and alone, best for her?"

"She belongs with her family."

"She belongs with you. Or are you getting cataracts in your old age blinding you to the fact the girl is nuts about you?"

"You just stated another reason. She's young. I'm not. She deserves a chance to explore and see the world. Date." He growled the word and only barely resisted punching the dash at the thought.

"Holy crap, I think all that lead in your body finally got to you. What a load of crock. All these excuses? They're meaningless and you know it. She loves you and you love her. And it scares the scales right off you."

"Does not," Viktor grumbled.

"Does too. You're afraid of loving her, afraid you won't make her happy and that she'll leave."

"I'm not a nice person."

"To your enemies. But to your friends and family, you're the best croc around. Or do you know a lot of bunnies who would call a cold blooded lizard their bestest friend?"

Viktor grimaced. "I knew I should have eaten her when I had the chance."

"Yes, you should have and saved us all."

"So I don't eat my friends, and maybe our age gap isn't so big. What about the fact I can't give Renee kids?"

A sad expression shadowed Mason's face. "No one can, buddy. Jessie decoded more of the hard drives from the lab. Renee, or should I call her Monique, is sterile. The scientists think the accident might have caused it. Whatever the cause, the end result is the same and you can't use it as an excuse."

It hurt Viktor to know his golden eyed vixen wouldn't have babes of her own. But at the same time, it meant there was one less barrier between them. "So what should I do? Dash up there and demand she leave her mother and come home with me?"

A laugh burst from Mason. "Maybe you should try for a little more subtlety. Go up there and tell her how you feel."

"Just blurt it out?"

"Nah. You're right. Not your style. Storm in, toss her over your shoulder, take her home and show her why she needs to stay."

Hmm, there was a plan with merit. But, for once, talk was needed more than action. "No. I won't seduce her into staying. I'll go talk to her, but if I end up dumped because I took your advice, I'm coming back to take it out on you."

Then he was slinking off to the swamp to lick his wounds in private.

*

Decided to get Viktor back, Renee didn't want to wait. She needed to find him now. She opened the door and saw the agents standing guard. "What happened to the other guards?"

"Suppertime," the cross eyed one replied. "What do you need?"

"Where's Viktor?"

"Alley. But our orders state you need to stay here."

"Too bad because I'm going outside."

"The boss won't like this," said the guard with the pinched face.

"She'll get over it. If you're so worried about my safety, then come with me, because I need to speak with him." And tell him she loved him and he wasn't getting rid of her that easily.

Stalking to the elevator, she pressed the button then waited, foot tapping. The doors slid open and she stepped in. With identical shrugs, her two guards joined her, but she really wished they would have showered before coming on duty. Then again, skunks never did smell pretty. She'd met enough of them during her time in the cells to know there wasn't a deodorant made that could dampen the smell.

Holding her breath, she counted floors as they descended. When the portal slid open her escorts stepped out first to scan the area. Deeming it clear, she followed them as they weaved through a series of corridors to the back alley.

Seeing the parked van with the tinted windows, she waved at them to stay back, not that they paid attention as they huddled together sharing a smoke. It surprised her. She'd gotten the impression FUC was tighter with its agents.

Not her problem. She skipped over to the vehicle. Before she could rap on the window it lowered but instead of the chiseled features she'd come to love, she saw Mason stuffing his face with a donut.

"Where's Viktor?" she asked peering around him to see the driver side sat empty.

"Gone upstairs to find you. But why are you with those two goons? I thought I assigned Jared and Carter to your door?"

She shrugged. "Apparently they're the dinnertime replacements. So Viktor came to find me? Do you know why?"

"Why do you think? Because he's an idiot who suddenly realized he was about to let the best thing that ever happened to him walk away."

"He said that?" She beamed.

"Not in so many words, but that's the gist."

"I better go find him."

Trotting back to her guards, she took the stairs this time, two at a time, until she reached the eleventh floor, huffing and puffing. No wonder Viktor stayed so fit. And to think he carried her the previous times he took the stairs. It explained where he got his stamina. And he thought he was too old.

Trotting down the hall, she didn't clue in something was wrong until she heard a pair of clicks behind her. Whirling, she saw her guards both pointing guns at her head.

"What's going on?"

"We're just the hired muscle following orders. You should ask the boss."

Who?

"Project, how nice to see you again."

Uh-oh. Pivoting slowly back around, Renee's heart stuttered to a stop as she saw the syringe poking Viktor's side. Hands in the air, he didn't seem at all concerned about the fact a crazy woman, who barely reached his waist, held him prisoner.

"Viktor! Are you alright? How's my mother?" she cried, fear making her frantic.

"Your mother is fine although she'll probably have a headache. I walked in before our little friend here could do any real damage. I promised to be a good croc if she left her alone."

175

"Little?" The mastermind gnashed her teeth and jabbed harder. "Quiet, lizard, or I'll forget my plan to use you to keep the fox in line."

"Plan? What plan? Why do you want him?"

"Well, I originally planned to hold your mother hostage for good behavior, but then your lover arrived while you went for a stroll. What better incentive could I have to make you follow orders than to capture him?" The mastermind smiled, and might have looked more menacing had her glasses not chosen to slide down to the tip of her nose.

"You can't do this. I won't let you."

"Don't worry about me, Renee. Just be ready to listen," he said cryptically. Viktor winked and she wondered if he'd gotten dust in his eye.

Despite his calm words, panic fluttered in her breast. "Let him go. You don't want him. You want me."

The woman, who'd held her prisoner for years, pushed up her thick glasses and smiled coldly. "But he is my security deposit. If you behave, he stays alive. If you don't…" Mastermind pushed the needle deeper. Viktor didn't flinch. On the contrary he looked bored.

Icy fear tickled her, followed by a slow rage.

"Calm, Renee," Viktor admonished. "Everything will work out fine. Trust me."

She did, but how would he escape? One push of the plunger and whatever vile concoction the mastermind brought would take her croc down.

It seemed like the mastermind didn't like his serene demeanor and words. "Move a muscle lizard, and Project gets it."

Still, Viktor didn't look worried.

"Why are you doing this?" Renee asked. "You escaped. You could have left and gone someplace where no one would know who you are. Started over."

"But I want the world to know me," squeaked the mastermind. "I am tired of hiding in cubby holes, scurrying in the darkness. I thought I finally had the answer, but something is missing. The formula didn't work. I need to try again, which means I need you."

Renee sighed. "Did it never occur to you that perhaps you're just not meant to be a gigantic carnivore?"

"If a bunny can grow great big teeth and a fox can outweigh an elephant, then so can I," said the mastermind stamping her little foot. "Now come along quietly or your croc will be doing a jiggle on the floor while foaming at the mouth."

"I'll come. I'll do anything you want, just don't hurt him. Please."

Viktor cocked his head. "Why? I'm just an old croc. Why give up your freedom for me?"

Did the drugs affect him already, rendering him stupid? "Because I love you, of course."

A smile spread across his face. "You do? Are you sure?"

"As sure as that damned sun will rise every day in the stupidly bright blue sky."

"Remember what I said about listening?" She nodded. "Duck," he yelled.

Acting before thinking, her instinct to obey coming naturally, she dropped to the floor and somehow still managed to see what happened next. Viktor lunged sideways away from Mastermind and her needle of poison. One of her guards fired a shot but missed Viktor who threw himself down and tucked into a roll, popping up in front of Renee. A pair of meaty thwacks later and the mastermind's minions snored beside Renee on the floor.

Helping Renee to her feet, Viktor had his back to the pint sized villain as he stroked the hair from her cheeks and smiled at her softly. With a snarl and a narrowing of big eyes behind overly large frames, the mastermind let out a scream as she ran, syringe held high.

"Viktor, watch out," Renee yelled.

Wham! Down went the villainess. Standing over her inert form, massive leather purse in hand, her mother sniffed. "Fool me once, shame on me. Fool me twice, and you will taste the wrath of my genuine alligator, leather purse."

Renee laughed as Viktor hugged her. They did it. She was free. The mastermind would end up behind bars. She would get to know her mother. She loved Viktor, but… Hold on a second. Did he love her back?

"Do you have something to tell me?" she asked when he leaned in to rest his forehead against hers.

"I'm glad you're safe?"

"No."

"Your mother has great aim?"

"No."

"I'm glad she went for gator instead of one of my distant croc cousins for the bag?"

"No. I told you I love you. Care to reply?"

"In front of everyone?" He looked appalled.

"It's just me, my mother and some unconscious villains."

"And me," said Mason exiting the stairwell, holstering his gun.

"And me," Kloe added exiting the room across the hall, sheathing her knives.

"Oh, just tell her before I sic Chase on you," Miranda hollered when she stuck her head out of yet another door.

"They were all here?" Renee asked.

"Of course. I wasn't taking any chances with your safety," Viktor said softly, tilting her chin up. "Because I protect those I love."

A chorus of 'Aaaah's made him cringe.

But Renee smiled so wide her face almost cracked. "Awesome. Now can we go home and have *dinner?*" Codespeak for his bed, without any clothes. He grinned toothily catching on.

"No one's going anywhere," a squeaky voice said. "Prepare to die!"

Chapter Twenty Three

Not again.

Viktor placed Renee behind him as the mastermind regained consciousness and threatened his fox. The villainess was truly delusional given she was surrounded by FUC agents.

"It's over, Mastermind. Hands up where we can see them," Kloe ordered with a rattle of silver cuffs.

The diminutive figure struggled to her knees. "Muahahahahahahahahahaha." The laughter started small, then increased in treble as the mastermind double, then tripled, then quadrupled in size.

Blinking, Viktor tried to mentally grasp the entity before him. A cross between a squirrel, a pygmy shrew – which for the uninformed was a cross between a mole and a tiny mouse – and a whole lot of monstrous Hyde, the mastermind burst out of her human skin into a veritable monster, replete with fangs, red eyes and a size on par with an elephant.

Unfortunately, the corridor wasn't meant for giant sized shifters and plaster rained down as the mastermind, tail slashing, arms thrashing, made room for her bulk. The haze of dust kick-started a chain of coughing and blinking as the FUC agents fought to breathe and see through the debris-caused murk.

Viktor didn't even have a chance to yell a warning to his vixen before a muscled tail, with a wicked barb on the end, wrapped around his middle, pinning his arms and sweeping him off the floor.

"Viktor!" He heard Renee's shrill cry, but he couldn't shout at her to run because he lacked the breath to do so, the crushing pressure on his rib cage stronger than he could fight. He tried to call his beast, even a half shift, but without oxygen, the most he managed was a spattering of scales.

Spots danced in front of his eyes and he wanted to curse the unfairness of dying when he'd just found out Renee loved him.

A roar shook the walls and he turned in time to see a bundle of red fur dive onto the mastermind's monstrous body. Once again, his fox came to his rescue. Good thing he was secure in his masculinity or he'd really have something to prove. On second thought, he'd schedule extra target practice next week on the range.

The tail released him and he tumbled to the floor. He didn't allow himself a chance to assess the damage to his ribs. Springing immediately to his feet, he cast a quick glance around for a weapon. Even he knew his croc was no match for the giant sized villainess, and Renee needed him.

"Viktor. Catch!" Miranda shouted and he whirled to catch the gun she tossed his way.

Spinning, he narrowed his eyes, focused on the tussling bodies causing havoc down the hall. Gashes scored Renee's body, bloody tears that turned his blood even colder than usual. He aimed, entering the zone. He fired. Once. Twice.

The red eyed, hybrid squirrel went limp, not that it stopped Renee from taking a bite and shaking her head with her mouthful. Then, with a toss of her massive, furry red head, she trotted back toward him, and he grinned. Damn, she was beautiful. And big. He'd have to make sure he stayed on her good side and took out the garbage. He wasn't sure he'd win in a wrestling match.

Plopping herself down in front of him, his vixen cocked her head and blinked her enormous golden eyes. A big tongue emerged to swipe him and Viktor grimaced. "We are going to have to talk about that."

Because he'd really rather she saved the licking for when it was the two of them, alone, and in human form. Then they could take turns.

Of course, pleasures of the erotic sort would have to wait until she managed to change back, which was hopefully soon seeing as how the commotion probably had the humans freaking on the lowers floors and the emergency departments for the city on their way.

Chaos ensued as they huddled and fleshed out a story. While Viktor managed to convince his fox to switch back by promising to let her ride cowgirl when they got home, they didn't have as much luck with the mastermind. In death, she retained her last shape, monstrous creation gone horribly wrong.

The authorities showed up and playing the part of terrified guests, the entire FUC gang along with Renee and her mother all stuck to the story that the creature came out of nowhere, scaring the hell out of them.

Damned sewer rats. They just kept getting bigger and bigger.

It didn't take long to escape the baffled cops, and with Madame Renarde sent to stay with Kloe for the night, Miranda hopping off with her hubby in tow because she needed some cheesecake to celebrate and Mason (who cared what that bear did?), it left Viktor alone at last with his vixen.

He couldn't get them home quick enough. She chattered the whole way.

"So do you think the police bought the story about it being some mutant rat?"

"They don't know what to believe."

"Won't they know when they test the corpse's DNA though?"

"It will never get that far. We have people in the right places to make sure the paperwork gets changed and the body accidentally cremated. In forty eight hours, the mastermind will cease to exist and our secret will be safe."

"Sooooo," she drew out the word. "Now what?"

Careening into the parking garage, and swerving into his spot, he didn't immediately reply. He jumped out of the loaner van, crossed over to her side and hauled her into his arms. When she would have spoken, he covered her lips with his.

"Mmmm." She hummed her appreciation.

But he wanted her screaming. Just not in the elevator where cameras watched. He contented himself with kissing her, pouring all of his feelings into the embrace. The fear he'd felt when he entered the hotel suite and saw Madame Renarde laid out on the floor, the helpless fury when he'd seen the goons point their guns at her head, his determination to save her at any cost, even his own life, and finally, pride in her because she loved him so much she took on the evil creature who tortured her for years.

Mixed in with all those emotions, he injected his love. Love for a red haired vixen who'd latched onto him with both hands – and sometimes even her legs – and wouldn't let go. She showed him what his life was missing. Her.

Entering his condo, he undressed Renee one-handed, the other balancing her against him. She giggled at his frenzy, but it also excited her, he discovered, when his hands slid between her thighs to find her slick and ready.

He tossed her on his bed and made quick work of his own garments, but when he would have crawled between her legs and feasted on her, she rolled away.

"Stop right there, crocodile. Someone promised me cowgirl."

"You remember that? I thought you didn't remember anything when the fox took over?"

"I don't. Or didn't, but for some reason, I distinctly recall you saying if I changed back, you'd teach it to me."

"Screw teaching. Nothing like hopping on top and learning from experience," he replied with a toothy grin. He stretched out on the bed, his cock jutting from his hips, loving how she perused him with glazed eyes.

She licked her lips and he twitched. "Save that for later. I want to be inside you. Now."

"Am I going to have to add impatience to your ornery nature?"

"How about insatiable, too, where you're concerned," he growled pulling her until she fell atop him. He caught her lips again and wouldn't let her pull away as she positioned herself over him. Her damp sex pressed against his lower stomach, and tension coiled inside him in anticipation of what would happen next. Sly vixen, she took her sweet time, lifting her bottom and dangling it over his cock, letting the tip of him brush her wet folds, but not sheathing him.

"Tease," he muttered against her lips.

"There goes that impatience again."

"We'll see how long your patience lasts when I torture you later."

"Promise?" she whispered.

"Anything you want. In case you haven't noticed, I can't resist you."

"Even though we can't have babies?" She'd admitted it to him while they waited for the cops to release them. He'd told her then he didn't care, but it didn't hurt to reassure her.

"I have more than enough nieces and nephews we can borrow. And there's always adoption."

"Or it could just be the two us. I think I'd like to have you all to myself."

"Well, you might have to loan me out once in a while for work."

"Maybe." Sitting down on him hard, encasing his cock in one fell swoop, he yelled and fisted the sheets. He heard her murmur, in a low growl, "Mine."

Grasping her hips, he helped her rock on top of him, catching her golden gaze with his own. "Yes, yours. I love you."

"Forever?"

"Even when I'm old and gray," he stated.

"Despite the fact my fox can kick your croc's ass?" she gasped, her fingers digging into his chest.

"Because you think you can."

She threw her head back and laughed as she rode him, a mirth that turned into pants of pleasure, then a cry of ecstasy as she came apart over him, on him. It was glorious.

Perfect.

Mine.

Forever…

Epilogue

Days later, after the quickest wedding in FUC history…

Toasty warm against Viktor's chest, mostly because her cold blooded husband built a huge fire, Renee – who found the name Viktor gave her more familiar than her birth name, Monique – sighed happily.

"What was that for?" Viktor asked cracking open an eye to peruse her.

"I can't believe we're on our honeymoon."

"Neither can I," he admitted in a wry tone.

"And thank goodness we lied about where we were honeymooning. I thought we'd never shake my mother. I didn't know someone could cry so much."

His chest rumbled with mirth. "You think yours was bad? I didn't know mine could cry at all. My getting married was not *that* shocking."

Renee snickered. "Tell that to the five hundred bucks I won in the office pool saying you wouldn't."

"Sly fox."

"Just living up to my roots." She laughed and ran a finger down his chest. The tip of it stopped at the edge of his newest scar. "Do you think it's really over?"

Viktor caught her hand and lifted it so he could place a kiss in the center. "The mastermind is gone. Her laboratories dismantled. The only thing you need to fear is…" He paused as if in thought. "Actually, I'll kill anything that scares you. I don't ever want to go through that kind of worry again."

"Me either. And just so you know, if anything ever threatens, or dares to flirt with you, I'll probably eat it."

"Because you're a bottomless pit."

"Am not," she giggled.

Okay, maybe she was, but lucky for her, she'd found a man who could cook up a storm, in and out of the bedroom. But his greatest skill of all – which almost tied with his ability to always hit the bulls-eye – was the love he held for her no matter her shape.

In the human world, the only time a croc and a fox got together was when a rich society matron carried one as a purse and the other as a fur stole. But in her world, the world of shifters, anything was possible, even a love between cold blooded and hot.

Or as Miranda liked to call them, Fozard. Which made no sense but drove Viktor nuts. And a Viktor ranting and raving was a lizard with his blood running hot. Yum.

*

The three a.m. phone call saw the good doctor shifting a snoring female body off him, and crawling over another. When the pride partied, no male lion ever went home alone, or with a single girl, whether he liked it or not.

Reaching his phone, he noted the FUC safe house number and answered. "Doctor Manners. What's wrong?"

"It's Fred."

"Fred who?"

"I'm one of the guards working the night shift at the safe house. You need to get over here, pronto. You know those folks we rescued?"

187

"Yeah. What about them? Is one of them having a seizure again?" Nolan asked as he located his pants and pulled them on.

"Kind of."

A bang echoed through the phone's receiver and he frowned.

"What was that?"

"One of your patients. Something's happening to them. They've gone crazy." The caller's breathing quickened in panic. "They're rampaging. The night nurse and the guard stationed with her are dead. I can't reach any of the others on duty. They've smashed the cameras so I can't see."

Bang! Bang! The reverberating sound of impact came through loud enough to mask the caller's frightened gasps.

"What's happening?" Nolan asked, icy fear tickling his spine.

"Shit. They're attacking the door."

The sound of the phone receiver hitting a hard surface didn't prevent Nolan from hearing the guard say, "Gary, get your gun out."

Nolan could only listen in stunned disbelief as the pounding increased, and then the more worrisome screech of bending metal came to his ears. As he texted FUC's main emergency line, he listened to the chaos. The snarling. The gun shots. The gurgling screams of terror.

Then the silence, the most worrisome sound of all. About to hang up, he jumped when a sibilant voice whispered into the phone. "Hello?"

A chill spread through him. "Who is this?"

"Who wants to know?" was the gruff rejoinder.

"It's Doctor Manners."

"Oh, hello, doc-tor. How nice of you to call. Won't you come and play? We're so awfully hungry and you always did smell so good."

No more Axe spray before work. Hell, maybe he'd skip showering too. "It sounds like you guys are in a spot of trouble. Let me help you."

"A doc-tor helping? As if." A bark of disdain followed.

Surely the victims the FUC team rescued saw the difference between the care from him and his staff compared to the torture suffered during their captivity. "I've never hurt you," Nolan said.

"You might not have hurt us like the rest, but you smell like *them*. We'll be seeing each other soon, doc-tor. Bloody soon." Crazy laughter, echoed by others in various pitches echoed shrilly from his ear pierce. Click. Dial tone.

Shit. That didn't bode well. Not well at all.

The End
(For now…Stay tuned for the next FUC story coming in 2013)

Author Biography

So you want to know a little about me? Well, I'm in my later thirties, married eleven years to a wonderful, supportive man—yes, he's a hunk—who gave me three beautiful, noisy children aged ten, seven, and five. I work as a webmistress and customer service rep from home, and in my spare time—of which there is tragically too little—I write, read, or Wii.

Wow, was that ever boring! Now for the fun stuff.

I'm writing romance the way I like it—hot with a touch of humor and spice. I tend to have a lot of sexual tension in my tales as I think all torrid love affairs start with a tingle in our tummies. My heroes are very male; you could even say borderline chest thumping at times, but they all have one thing in common; an everlasting love and devotion to their woman.

Visit me on the Web for news on current and upcoming releases at

http://www.EveLanglais.com

Thanks for reading.